Old Dog

Also by Roy F. Chandler

- All About a Foot Soldier (A colorful book for children)
- History of Early Perry County Guns and Gunsmiths (With Donald L. Mitchell)
- A History of Perry County Railroads
- Alaskan Hunter: a book about big game hunting
- Kentucky Rifle Patchboxes and Barrel Marks
- Tales of Perry County
- Arrowmaker
- Hunting in Perry County
- Antiques of Perry County
- The Black Rifle
- Homes, Barns and Outbuildings of Perry County
- Shatto
- The Perry County Flavor
- Arms Makers of Eastern Pennsylvania
- The Didactor
- Fort Robinson: A novel of Perry County PA, the years 1750-63
- Friend Seeker: A novel of Perry County PA
- Gunsmiths of Eastern Pennsylvania
- Perry County in Pen & Ink
- Shatto's Way: A novel of Perry County, Pa
- Chip Shatto: A novel of Perry County Pennsylvania, the years 1863-6
- Pennsylvania Gunmakers (a collection)
- Firefighters of Perry County
- The Warrior, A novel of the frontier
- Perry County Sketchbook (And Katherine R. Chandler)
- A 30-foot, $6,000 Cruising Catamaran, 1987
- The Gun of Joseph Smith (With Katherine R. Chandler)
- The Perry Countian,
- Hawk's Feather - An Adventure Story
- Ted's Story
- Alcatraz: The Hardest Years 1934-1938 (With Erville F. Chandler)
- Cronies
- Song of Blue Moccasin
- Chugger's Hunt

- The Sweet Taste
- Tiff's Game: A work of fiction
- Tuck Morgan, Plainsman (Vol. 2) (With Katherine R. Chandler)
- Death From Afar I (And Norman A. Chandler)
- Kentucky Rifle Patchboxes All New Volume 2
- Behold the Long Rifle
- Death From Afar II: Marine Corps Sniping (And Norman A. Chandler)
- Old Dog
- Tim Murphy, Rifleman: A novel of Perry County, Pa. 1754-1840
- Choose the Right Gun
- Death From Afar Vol. III: The Black Book (And Norman A. Chandler)
- The Kentucky Pistol
- Ramsey: A novel of Perry County Pennsylvania
- Gray's Talent
- Hunting Alaska
- Last Black Book
- Dark Shadow (The Red book series)
- Death From Afar IV (And Norman A. Chandler)
- Morgan's Park (Vol. 3) (With Katherine R. Chandler)
- White Feather: Carlos Hathcock USMC scout sniper (And Norman A. Chandler)
- Death From Afar V (And Norman A. Chandler)
- Ironhawk: A frontier novel of Perry County Pennsylvania 1759-1765
- Sniper One
- One Shot Brotherhood (And Norman A. Chandler)
- Shooter Galloway
- The Hunter's Alaska
- The Boss's Boy
- Pardners
- Hawk's Revenge
- Blackwater Jack

OLD DOG

A Novel of Perry County, Pennsylvania

Roy F. Chandler

This is a work of fiction. The major characters in this book and the situations depicted are the author's creation. They did not exist or happen.

Old Dog. Copyright © 2017 by Katherine R. Chandler. All rights reserved.

First printing: 1993. Bacon and Freeman, Publishers

Cover art by the author. Book design by John Booth.

Chapter 1

The doctor looked his age. At seventy his well-barbered jowls rounded his features but did not disguise the bag of eyes or sag of skin beneath a once formidable jaw. Comfortable self-indulgence and good living had thickened him into a jovial Saint Nicholas, whose eyes could twinkle and crease with the pleasures of life.

His patient was a decade younger, with ropy-muscled arms and lean legs. His long dour features resembled those of actor Sam Elliot, and his thickly salt and peppered hair hung to his shoulders, as the movie star's often did.

The overweight physician was in good health. His tough and wiry patient was dying.

They were friends—had been since the Korean fighting forty years past—and, despite his years in medicine with countless other patients, Doctor Phil Klein could never lose the memory of those first meetings. They had been young and strong then, with the world waiting—if they could survive the killing grounds north of the Pusan perimeter.

In 1951, MASH units had not become popularized on film and in television. Mobile Army Surgical Hospitals practiced medicine as close to the front lines as possible. MASH doctors fought to save lives and limbs.

Their surgery was necessarily fast and dirty—patch up whatever was life threatening and evacuate the patients to a distant hospital where time and equipment to finesse were available. Or, sew 'em up, shoot 'em full of penicillin, and hustle them back to their units.

The first time they met, Sergeant "Dog" Carlisle was one of those destined to return to his combat outfit.

Captain Phil Klein could be annoyed by patients like Sergeant Carlisle. Even in the damp sweat of shock and pain, soldiers like Carlisle urged the surgeon to hurry so they could get back to their outfits.

Most wounded prayed and occasionally pleaded for evacuation—to be finally and officially free of the horrors of infantry war. Their hunger was normal (who would not want to be out of it?) and Doctor Klein could empathize.

The ones eager to get back into combat were harder to appreciate, but Doc Klein tried because understanding might help make the slaughter and maiming a hint more tolerable.

Something sharp had sliced along Sergeant Carlisle's ribs. It had cut deep, scraping bone before parting some of the latissimus muscle under the left arm. It was a long gash, perhaps nine inches, and as clean as if done with a straight razor. The wound bled copiously until Klein's sutures closed its gaping mouth. Not life threatening or genuinely crippling, but the Sergeant would still be laid up nearly a month before the muscle was sufficiently reknit for physical exertion.

Klein had said, "Carlisle, huh? Named after the writer or the town in Pennsylvania?" If he had considered, Captain Klein might not have suggested that an army infantry noncom would be conversant with the noted Thomas Carlyle, a Victorian author included in literary canon.

The Sergeant's breath hissed a little as Klein drew a suture. "Thomas isn't a relative, but I am from Perry County, a little north of the city of Carlisle. I never heard that we were related there either."

The doctor had a conversational handle. "Well, well, neighbor. I'm from Harrisburg. I've worked on a lot of Perry County hoop polers."

"What's your name again, Doc?"

"Klein, Philip, no middle initial. I'm with Harrisburg Hospital." The doctor snipped the last stitch and sat back to examine his work.

"Can't recall the name, sir."

"Well, keep me in mind after you're home. I'm in the book. Never can tell when someone'll fall off a thresher or get kicked by a steer and need a surgeon with the golden touch."

"Everybody in Perry County isn't a farmer, Captain." The sergeant was quick with his defense.

Klein grinned disarmingly, then stuck in another barb. "Of course not Sarge, but since the CCC and the WPA closed down, there isn't much going on up in them-thar-hills."

The sergeant attempted to sit up, but Klein laid on a restraining hand. "Just stay down, neighbor. You've lost a lot of blood, and plasma isn't quite the same. You'll probably be a little woozy. The orderlies will get you cleaned up and into a comfortable sack. A pain pill will put you to sleep, and in the morning we'll evacuate you back to Japan for a few weeks."

Carlisle said, "Oh hell," and again moved to sit up.

"Damn it, Sergeant, stay down."

"Captain, I've got to get back to my platoon. You don't understand. There's no lieutenant, and I don't have a noncom who's been in the army a full year."

"No, Sarge, *you* don't understand. You won't lift that arm for at least a week, and it won't be fit to use for more weeks. You are out of it, and that's that!" Doc Klein had learned that being decisive and in charge did best with military people.

For a long moment the sergeant stayed rigid under Klein's hand. Then he relaxed. His voice was resigned. "OK, Doc, this is your outfit."

Suspicious of the swift capitulation, Klein called an orderly. "Get the patient cleaned up. He smells like a goat. Take his clothing; leave only his personals. He'll get reissued in Japan."

Carlisle said, "Damn it, leave my boots. I can't sleep without knowing where my boots are."

Klein sighed, "Leave the boots."

"I keep my personals in my boot. I don't want my wallet packed away somewhere."

"Your gear will be in your boots, Sarge." The orderly had learned not to sweat the small stuff. Line soldiers could be weird. They could get pissed over nothing, and it paid to give them a little slack when you could.

No other casualties were waiting so Klein took extra moments. He flipped through the Sergeant's thin medical record. Intrigued, he said, "Dog Carlisle? Your first name is Dog?" He leaned across to read Carlisle's identification tag.

"Says here your name is Adam B. Carlisle."

"Well, everybody calls me Dog, Captain. So that's what I go by."

"Adam sounds a hell of a lot better than Dog."

"I like Dog."

Klein slapped the metal form holder closed and wedged it between his patient's calves. He looked closely at Carlisle's worn and muddied combat boots. "If it were me, I'd be glad to get rid of those rotten old boots and get new ones."

"They're just broken in, Captain. New boots are hell up on the line."

"Well, you won't have to worry about that for a while."

Klein watched the orderlies ease his patient onto a stretcher.

As they started out he added, "Dog. What a hell of a nickname. You hoop polers have strange ideas. I know a Bung, a Tater, and a Crunch from up there. There's probably something in the Perry County well water that affects you all."

Klein grinned to himself, but Dog Carlisle wasn't done quite yet.

"There's an old Perry saying you ought to keep in mind, Captain. It goes, 'If Perry County didn't have sewers, Harrisburg couldn't draw their rations.'"

The screened doors swung closed behind the litter bearers.

Sergeant Carlisle said, "I've got a jeep driver waiting out here. Give me a minute to send him home, OK?"

"Sure, Sarge. What's his name?"

"Corporal Cole."

They found Cole in the mess hall and brought him, sandwich in hand.

"Geez, Dog. This outfit eats like kings. Move over and I'll stay here with you."

Carlisle motioned the ward boys away. "What I've got to tell Corporal Cole is classified. It'll only take a minute." The sergeant spoke softly to the corporal, who nodded repeated understanding.

They clasped hands, and the sergeant warned, "Don't screw up, Cole."

"No sweat, Sarge. Take care of yourself." He saluted with his sandwich and departed.

Cleaned up and fed well, with his wounds bandaged and a restrainer from elbow to waist so that he could not lift his arm too high, Sergeant Dog Carlisle was eased between sheets and given the prescribed pain pill. His boots with his wallet and watch stuffed in were aligned militarily beneath his cot. The medical record was hung from the foot of the bunk, and the ward boys attended to other duties.

Ten minutes later, Dog sat up. He shook his head attempting to clear the cobwebs of sedative and blood loss. Using only his good arm, he fumbled into his boots and hung his wallet from the cotton drawstring of his hospital pajamas.

"You supposed to be up?" The soldier in the next cot was concerned.

"Yeah, I've just got a gash along the ribs. I'm just going to the latrine." Dog worked at his watchband.

"Don't use the commode on the end. The seat's cracked, and it'll pinch like a lobster."

"Thanks. War is hell, isn't it?"

"I like it better today than yesterday?"

"Know what you mean. Go to sleep. I'll be right back."

Dog wove an unsure way down the bunk line. He eased quietly through the ward door and headed for the screened-off patients' latrine.

Corporal Cole was waiting as directed.

"Where in hell have you been, Dog? I've hung around here so long people are looking at me funny."

"Where's the jeep?"

"About a hundred yards through here." Cole led the way.

Dog dropped into the passenger seat. "Let's go." He slumped deep, wedging his knees against the dash.

"I'm going to sleep. They gave me a knock-out pill, and I'm low on blood, so if I start to fall out grab me. Wake me when we get there."

"OK, Sarge. Cripes, I hope I don't get my butt in a sling over this. You're AWOL now, you know."

"Who cares? Get driving."

Battalion supply found Sergeant Carlisle's duffel bag. He got out clean fatigues and drew a steel helmet. The company armorer would still have his Ml rifle and belted forty-five pistol.

"Hey, Dog, you're supposed to be carrying a carbine. Not that I give a s---, but I'm supposed to account for these guns."

"If I see the carbine around, I'll send it back. Might as well throw rocks as shoot with a carbine."

The armorer was disdainful. "You'll hit more with a carbine than this damned pistol. Where'd you get this, anyway? It isn't on our records.

"It just showed up. I'll will it to you."

The Sergeant Major was waiting.

"Glad you're back, Dog. You didn't look so good going out."

The Sergeant Major studied Dog more carefully. "You still look like hell. You all clear with the medics?"

"I'm here, Top. I just bled a lot." A strategic shift of subject. "Sounds quiet up front."

"Been quiet, but there's a lot of stirring going on. Something's brewing."

"I need a lift to company."

"Sit down a while. Your CO is coming back, and the Colonel wants to see you."

"I'll sack out in supply, Sarge. I can use the sleep. Call me when I'm needed."

They were not formal. The Captain said, "I need a lieutenant, Dog. You are it. Don't give me a lot of bull about not wanting to be an officer. I haven't got time for it."

The Battalion Commander said, "You'll do a good job, Lieutenant Carlisle."

Dog said, "I'm not sure . . . "

The Sergeant Major said, "Shut up, Dog, and raise your right hand for the oath."

Captain Phil Klein was notified that his patient was gone.

"Gone? Hell, he can't be far. He got his pill, didn't he? Then he's asleep somewhere around here."

"We figure his jeep driver waited for him, sir. The patient next to Carlisle said we no more than walked out when he put his boots on and left. Said he was going to the latrine. Hell, he'd just been there. Anyway, he never came back.

"He's gone to his outfit, Captain."

Klein knew the orderly was right.

"Have the duty officer call his unit. Have Carlisle picked up and brought back. Make them understand he is not fit for duty. God, what next?" Doctor Phil Klein was genuinely exasperated.

"Sergeant Major Graff here, Sir? I am returning your duty officer's call concerning a Sergeant Adam B. Carlisle?

"Yes, Sir. I have personally checked our battalion roster, and we have no enlisted or noncommissioned officers named Carlisle.

"Yes, Sir. I am one hundred percent positive that no Sergeant Carlisle is assigned to this organization or is serving here unassigned.

"Thank you, Sir. You are right that we cannot have patients unaccounted for. I hope you find your man."

The Sergeant Major hung up, satisfied that he would not be called again. Both MASH and battalion had other problems to handle.

The Sergeant Major had not lied. He never did. Now if MASH had asked about a Lieutenant Carlisle, the answers would have been different, but the medics would still have struck out. Old Dog was back on the line and doing his job. Sometimes the medics forgot that their duty was to support the infantry, not to ship every flesh wound back to the States.

Chapter 2

Vicious combat burdened Klein's MASH unit. As fighting edged north, the hospital moved, then traveled far with the Allied advance up the peninsula. AWOL patients were reported and forgotten. New emergencies appeared, were dealt with and, like Sergeant Dog Carlisle, virtually forgotten.

Heat of summer sloughed into fall, and winter cold bit its first warnings. Major Phil Klein's Korean tour was winding down. A replacement surgeon was en route. When he reappeared, Klein would pack a few belongings and depart. Hammered by too many tension-packed surgeries, numbed and disgusted by the seemingly endless streams of torn young men, Klein was more than ready to go home. As powerfully as any other battered combat veteran, Doc Klein wanted to see the last of Korea.

To the north, a bitter fire fight exploded. American artillery responded, shaking the MASH tents and jarring mental concentration. Fighters were seen diving on not-too-distant targets, and a pair rushed close overhead, their thunder shattering nerves and leaving a wake of curses and racing hearts.

Casualties began as a trickle and, as usual, grew quickly into a flood. MASH was the first stop behind the lines. Helicopters and jeeps delivered. Ambulances and helicopters moved the treated further rearward.

Wounded and broken bodies were identified, tagged, and hastily diagnosed. Doctors stayed in place and new patients were trundled to the hastily-sterilized medical tables. The surgeons treated wounds to stop bleeding, to stabilize condition, and to prevent death. They barely examined faces, much less the feelings of those they worked over. There was no time. Other sufferers waited and real hospitals, beyond the rush of outbound artillery, would observe the niceties of the doctor/patient relationship.

A nurse pointed to an angry-appearing hole in a lean patient's chest. "Bullet went in here." Nurse and surgical tech rolled the unresisting casualty onto his side. "And came out there." A wrist-sized exit wound seeped a little blood.

"The wound isn't sucking."

"Isn't bleeding much either. May not have nicked a lung."

"Blew some of the scapula out the back."

"Nothing big seems to be bleeding."

"Lucky man."

"Probably." Klein looked for further damage. On the patient's left side a long scar, fairly recent, showed crude and imaginative stitching and restitching.

Klein said, "Wait a minute!" He looked close, studying the drawn, dirty, and unshaven features.

Dog said, "Hey, Doc, it's been a while."

"Adam Carlisle!" The name came surprisingly easy to Klein's memory. "What happened this time?"

Though groggy from a medic's morphine, Carlisle answered clearly enough. "Got shot, Doc." His mouth quirked in amusement. "I'm pretty sure it was the enemy."

"Well, you're lucky a second time. The bullet seems to have missed a lot of important pieces."

"Good to hear. Feels like my whole side's gone numb."

"It'll wear off and you'll wish it was back. You won't be sneaking off on us this time, Sergeant.

"Lieutenant," the nurse corrected.

"Lieutenant?" Klein's eyebrows rose. "You've gone down in the world, Dog."

"They needed someone to draw fire, Doc."

The nurse snickered and a surgical tech laughed openly.

The team began work.

Klein said, "We'll put you to sleep now, Carlisle. I probably won't see you again. You'll wake up in a ward and be hustled out of the zone from there. Come visit me in Harrisburg. I'll be home before you are."

The doctor stayed the anesthesiologist's hand. "One more thing, Dog. What in hell happened to your first wound? I didn't do that sewing."

Dog grunted in uncomfortable amusement. "Damned thing kept tearing open. Our medic got some sutures and resewed it a few times. Finally healed up all right."

While his patient was prepped, Klein mused about it. Tougher than tripe, he thought. A lot of the Perry County people that ended up seeing him were like that. If a horse kicked their faces in, they wrapped a rag around whatever was broken and got back to work. Farmers were brought in carrying a piece of hand or some fingers, wondering if he could sew the parts back on—anxious to get back to bailing "before it rained on the hay."

Perry Countians were known as rugged people. Provincial as hell, they fought, loved, and married each other. If you weren't born there, you never could really be one.

The Dog Carlisles were the heart and muscle of the American military. They went in and did whatever had to be done. Then they went home and, with little fanfare, took up where they had left off. Tough, often semi-educated, God-fearing Americans—Phil Klein guessed the country would be crippled and weak without them.

Lieutenant Carlisle had known it was coming. Intelligence reported communist troops massing, and air strikes worked on them. Before dawn, too many lights (of cigarettes, flashlights, even lanterns) glittered before dousing, and engines were detected by listening posts.

Light had barely broken when trumpets and whistles sounded behind the first ridge. Artillery began landing within American barbed wire and mined approaches. Friendly fire rustled overhead and thundered down unseen, hopefully among the enemy preparing to strike.

When they came, the earth seemed to march. A solid wash of green and brown uniformed, pressed-together humanity surged over the ridgeline, flowed across the low ground, and rose upward like a tide into the hail of American rifle and machine gun fire.

Dog Carlisle had his men ready. Mines would help, and their barbed wire was good. Both would channel the enemy into the final protective fires of his machine guns. His platoon's three Browning automatic rifles were on line, and the squads were deployed in well-dug two-man foxholes. He had the weapons platoon on sound-powered phone, and the 60mm mortars were pre-zeroed to dump hard and fast on a number of probable trouble spots.

There was a lot more.

Artillery was already pounding the attack, and battalion had their 81mm mortars and recoilless rifles working. Those weapons ranged all along the front. They could devastate, but Dog knew through experience that despite the intensity of artillery, even aerial napalm strikes, the North Korean and Red Chinese would keep coming. It was claimed that if they faltered, their own officers would execute them. Dog doubted most of that, but for whatever reasons, the Reds came hard.

Smoke clouded visibility. Dog's riflemen began firing too hastily. Squad leaders scurried, settling the fire, even as enemy mortar shells began raining on their positions. Then the enemy reached them. Wave-like, they flung themselves ahead. Bodies crushed the concertina wire and flattened the double apron fences. Dog's machine guns tore and ripped enemy uniforms into unmoving piles. Friendly mortars and artillery fell into the churning mass, so close that fragments whistled among the defenders.

The enemy was through and among them. Dog dropped the friendly fire as close as permitted, and the reserve platoon behind Dog's line began a ripple of shots that almost instantly exploded into a roaring blast of supporting gunfire.

Lieutenant Dog Carlisle became a rifleman. Enemy infantrymen appeared behind his squad lines, and Dog began killing them. He fired swiftly, but taking the extra instant necessary to find his target. More appeared, seeming to rush blindly ahead, not bothering even to fire into the foxholes they were passing.

Dog slapped home a fresh clip, aware of his radio man's rifle thumping beside him. He cleared targets in front of them, but others ran past. Dog snatched his pistol, and its recoil jarred his hand.

He felt the enemy weakening. More than seeing, Dog sensed the disintegration of the charge. Fire slackened almost as quickly as it had begun. Then it again rose, lacing retreating enemy while targets remained visible. Gradually the firing dribbled away to individual shots. Observers were moving artillery and mortar fire away, back down the slope, pounding the enemy's withdrawal. Dog holstered his empty pistol and fought a loaded clip into his hot-barreled Ml rifle.

The radio operator kept repeating, "Holy God! Holy God!"—as if he were amazed that they had survived. Dog Carlisle felt the same. It had been close and brutal. Bodies sprawled, and the cries of wounded rose amid the rumble of receding artillery.

Partly deafened and physically drained, his mind numb and barely responsive, Dog battled himself alert, to take stock, to regroup. To counterattack? To surge down the hill with his surviving remnants, to drive the beaten enemy across the open, over the ridge, and through their own positions—how could they manage? But, the order might come.

Dog called to a squad leader busy with wounded. A pair of medics scrambled by, and the sound-powered phone began buzzing. The radio operator held out his handpiece. "Old Man is on."

Dog said, "Lieutenant Carlisle, Captain. We're in one piece. I'll . . .

The bullet struck him with a huge hollow booming impact that seemed to balloon somewhere inside him. There was an instant of—What the hell? Before he knew he had been shot. Dog saw his left arm out-flung for some unrecognized reason. He felt his knees against the side of his hole, and then his face was down on the parapet, and he heard his radio operator calling, "The Lieutenant's hit!"

Dog was embarrassed. He was unceremoniously rolled onto his back and his upper clothing ripped away. The medic kept saying, "Son-of-a-bitch," with metronomic regularity as he labored. Someone was bellowing for a stretcher, and all Dog could do was lie like an empty shell casing while the tasks went on.

The medic got plastic on him—you tried to stop a chest wound from sucking air. Then the corpsman stabbed a morphine syrette into him but there was no pain, just a monumentally huge numbness, as though most of his left side had been hollowed out and only the skin left in place.

He was on a stretcher. The medic had a tag on him telling when morphine had been given.

The medic leaned close, and Dog could smell his cigarette breath. "You're OK, Lieutenant. Not even bleeding much." Then the bearers lifted, and Dog saw the medic dash away.

They had won, fought off the enemy at least. Artillery whispered overhead, but the impacts were far away. Friendly uniforms were arriving, and Dog got his head up to see enemy dead or wounded lumped in ungainly piles and sprawled throughout the position. His radioman waved an encouraging hand, and Dog saw his Platoon Sergeant moving in to take command.

The effort to think and see exhausted him. Dog collapsed in on himself, only half aware of the bearer's struggles across the chewed and broken terrain. On the reverse slope of their ridge, Korean bearers took over and seemed to do better.

A needle stung his arm, and Dog was aware of a saline or maybe a plasma bag dangling above him. Looking harassed and too busy to linger, his Captain said a few encouraging words.

The flump-flump of helicopter blades caught his hearing, and he hoped he wasn't being given first treatment because he was an officer.

The ride was barely up and down. MASH units stayed close. White coats appeared, and words were said. Orders passed, but he probably slept a little.

Dog couldn't recall the doctor's name, but the face came clear through the narcotic fog, and Dog felt suddenly in good hands. He was barely aware of their conversation. As an anesthesia cone closed over his nose and mouth, he hoped he had not sounded slow and stupid. He sure wasn't feeling as sharp as usual.

Chapter 3

Doctor Philip Klein had again drifted Dog Carlisle from his thoughts. Home, courting a friend of long acquaintance and nourishing a growing medical practice absorbed Klein's attention. He doctored, dated, and worked out at the YMHA for nearly a year before Adam Carlisle reappeared.

"Doctor, there is a young man insisting on seeing you."

"Send him down the hall. No patients on surgery day."

"He says you are his doctor."

Klein was almost impatient.

"It doesn't . . ."

"Something about Korea, Doctor." The secretary saw Klein's attention sharpen and looked to her notes. "His name is odd. Dog Carlisle."

Klein sat back in his chair. "Well I'll be blasted. The Lazarus of our latest war."

The secretary appeared confused.

"Lazarus, Miss Hawn. A man gentiles believe was raised from the dead.

"Oh."

"Show him in." Then suspiciously, "He isn't bleeding, is he?"

"No, at least not much, but he is all scraped up and he . . ." Klein went past her through the door.

Scraped was an understatement. Dog Carlisle appeared to have been dragged behind stallions.

Motorcycle wreck! Klein knew the signs—leather jacket road-rashed almost through; hands and knees skidded into raw meat; and one side of the face scratched and oozing blood. Apparently, no head injuries, although the victim stood funny. Classic motorcycle trauma.

Dog said, "Hey, Captain, it's me again."

"I made major, Carlisle." Klein waved toward a treatment room. "Get in there."

Dog limped, favoring a knee, and he held his left forearm tight to his chest. Kline called for assistance, and a nurse hurried in.

The leather jacket had to be eased off because Dog's left arm hurt badly.

Klein said, "We ought to cut it off."

"Easy, Doc, it'll come. This jacket cost seventy-five bucks."

"Then you should have taken care of it. I could read a paper through the elbows."

"I'll sew on patches." Clad only in his boxer shorts, Dog sat on the edge of the examination table.

"Where are you hurt?"

"Left shoulder aches like hell, and my left knee pains and is swelling. The scratches don't matter."

Klein snorted. "Don't matter? Skin matters, and you've ground a lot of it off."

The doctor touched the healed over bullet wounds on Dog's chest and back. "Nice work there."

"Yeah, a surgeon in Tokyo fixed it up."

Klein's lips quirked. He doubted the wound had been opened since he had cleaned and stitched.

The shoulder did not take long. "Collar bone's broken, Dog. I can feel the movement."

Dog's breath whistled. "Damn, so can I. Quit wiggling it around."

"Quiet! Sergeants don't talk back to majors."

"I made lieutenant"

"I forgot that. Come to think about it, this is the first time I've seen you upright." Klein examined his patient critically. "Thought you'd be taller."

The knee required X-raying, but Klein was optimistic. "My guess is your knee just twisted a little too much, and it'll heal itself. Let's hope so. We can't do much with bad knees. You ought to stay off motorcycles. Damned things should be outlawed."

"I was doing fine until some fool pulled out in front of me. I went over the curb avoiding him, lost control, and skidded along the sidewalk. Bent my fork, dented the tank, and broke my headlight. The car driver never knew anything had happened. He just drove on happy as a clam."

"Where was this?"

"On Front Street, almost down to Market."

"So, you just walked on down here. Why didn't you go to Emergency?"

Dog appeared surprised. "Why would I do that, knowing you worked here? In Emergency I'd get some intern still learning about adhesive tape."

Logical! Klein muttered, "I don't have patients wandering in. I'm a surgeon, not a general practitioner."

Dog was unfazed. "I follow the Chinese principle of medicine."

"What principle? Probably tea leaves and pin sticking."

"The principle that if you save a life you are responsible for its presence from then on."

Klein grimaced. "If I'd known that I'd have passed you to another cutter."

The doctor watched the nurse scrubbing and picking at Dog Carlisle's abrasions.

"You'll have to have your arm strapped down for a couple of weeks to let that clavicle set. Assuming nothing is chipped in your knee, you can soak it in your bathtub . . . "

"I'm a shower man."

"Shut up, Dog. Soak your knee and try to keep the filth out of all these raw places. Keep 'em protected and give them a chance to grow new skin."

Klein again looked suspicious. "You aren't mucking around in barnyards or anything, are you?"

"Not me, Doc. Right now I'm staying home, waiting for opportunity to knock."

"Good! Stay home, listen to the radio, and use the ointment. Those are orders."

"Yes, sir, Major, sir!"

That had been back in . . . oh, in the middle 1950's, the doctor mused. Dog had shown up with some regularity since then. Now, here they were, old men, friends for some forty years. Forty years . . . it seemed like yesterday.

Unlike earlier times, Doctor Phil Klein had no good news for his friend and patient. This was not a bullet wound or a broken bone to square away. Dog Carlisle had cancer. The disease had metastasized. It was devouring

Dog's innards. Cancer was flourishing in his bone marrow, and it was clogging his lymph system. Except for pain control there was nothing sensible medical science could do about it.

Yet, Old Dog looked good. Most cancer victims passed through a point where fat had melted away and features looked young and taut. The healthy appearance did not last, of course. To the trained eye, the leaned-down look spoke of imminent demise. Usually it was cancer, but some AIDS patients also experienced the "looking good" phase.

Physical appearance was often deceptive, and in terminal cases like Dog Carlisle's, it could sometimes raise false hopes. Some patients were helped by false expectations. They required all the support, legitimate or otherwise, that could be mustered. Old Dog Carlisle was not one of those.

Klein sighed heavily and pushed back in his squeaky old swivel chair. His hands gestured expressively. Resignation as well as distress were clear in the body language.

"There is no argument, Dog. Every symptom, every test, every opinion agrees. It's as clear-cut as any case I've encountered.

Klein slapped the padded chair arms in frustration. "I'd give anything to have it otherwise."

Old Dog nodded acceptance, sighing in turn and exhaling in his own resignation. Still, he asked. "No radiation or chemotherapies, Phil?" They had passed name formalities decades earlier.

"Oh hell, Dog. We could go through all the treatments. Some think it's a doctor's duty. More than a few oncologists believe in straw grasping, and I've got to admit the occasional miracle does appear.

"But, Dog, the medical miracles are so rare they about equal the magical cures of those who choose to do nothing. We can shoot you full of the best stuff available and nuke you till you glow in the dark, but the truth is we won't cure and we probably won't even delay.

"What is sure as taxes is that whatever time you've got left will be miserable. Stiff chemo can make you so sick you'll wish you were dead, and radiation—especially in the doses they would be beaming into you—could be as bad."

"Would you try it, if you were me, Phil?"

The answer was swift and as positive as Klein could make it.

"No! I wouldn't let them touch me."

"What would you do?"

This answer was harder, and the doctor leaned back to think a little.

"I'm sure of only part of it, Dog. I'd keep myself pain free . . . and I'll take good care of you there, old friend. There is no need for god-awful suffering these days. We've got powerful painkillers, and I believe in using them.

"What would I do beyond that? Enjoy myself, I think. Maybe I'd travel, but, maybe not. Most, it seems to me, just keep on doing pretty much what they've always done, as long as they can. Familiar things appear to become more important and comforting than seeing new places. That makes some sense to me.

Old Dog asked the big question. He had asked before. Hell, they had gone over all of this more than once, but it still seemed necessary to hear it again.

"How long have I got? The best you can guess, Phil."

The doctor did not have to ponder an answer. He had evaluated and judged, as well as guessed, until he knew the best response.

"You won't have more than three months on your feet, Dog, and some of that won't be pleasant. You'll have to dope up heavier all the time to keep the pain down. That'll leave you woozy; you'll sleep a lot, and you'll lose track of time.

"Once you are down, it'll just be a matter of pain control till you die. How fast that will be is harder to guess. More months, probably."

The doctor hated his words. "God, Dog, I wish I could say something encouraging, but it isn't there."

"I know, Doc, I know. Sorry to put you through telling it again, but I wanted one more assurance. I've got it set now, and I know how I'll handle myself."

Carlisle paused, raising his eyes to hold those of the doctor's. "You know how I feel about dying slowly, Phil. I'm not doing it."

"I understand, Dog. Hell, I agree, and I've got my own plans." The doctor struggled for words.

"I'm pleased you're planning carefully, Dog. I've known too many who liked to claim they'd just shoot themselves before they would suffer, but they never did. They waited too long and lost will, or their religion loomed up and scared them off. A man has to have a serious plan and have what he needs ready. If he doesn't, he will end up letting nature and medical science fight it out. That can get really lousy, Dog."

"I'm a Hemlock Society member. I intend to use their methods."

"Fair enough. I've read their literature. When you are ready, I'll have the stuff. Pick it up early, Dog. Don't wait until the last minute. You might misjudge, and in a hospital, living wills and powers of attorney won't do what you want."

"I'll pick it up in a couple of weeks. Right now, I'm functioning, and I've got things that I need doing."

"Call me, Dog. If I don't hear regularly, I'm going to call you."

"I'll be down, Phil, and soon."

Chapter 4

He might be dying . . . hell, he was dying. It was time to dump the maybes, but at the moment, Dog felt decent. A sort of dull, barely-noticeable ache lay somewhere deep in his guts. It was always there, sometimes flaring, but still tolerable most of the time.

It was a special February day. Brisk but spring-like weather had been cropping up a lot in recent winters. Years back, Februarys had always been bitter, an ice and snow month important to miss if you could make it down to Florida.

A pair of young boys crouched beside the parked Harley-Davidson, staring raptly at the bright chrome and mystery-black paint job. Unnoticed, Old Dog watched them, zipping high his leather jacket and closing the zippers on forearms. He gripped his battered black helmet between his knees and tugged on padded riding gloves that sported stiff gauntlets extending well beyond his wrists. They kept the cold wind from running up the jacket sleeves.

Unlike most riders, Dog did not wear engineer or cowboy boots. In their place he chose the tight-ankled protection of old style army paratroop boots. Fitted with lug soles, they wore long when skidded against road pavement.

Leather chaps protected Dog's legs from cold wind and displayed a number of silver conchos crudely hammered from Mexican coins. Cinched at the waist by a broad leather belt, the chaps lent their wearer a touch of cowhand and completed the almost armored appearance of a Harley-Davidson motorcycle rider.

Dog asked, "Like her looks, men?"

The boys were uninhibitedly enthusiastic. They threw together sounds of approval. "Really rad" and "Ultimate" were among them. Dog could feel their silent envy and admiration as he straddled his machine.

The leather saddle was cold against his denims as he snugged his helmet and tightened the chin strap. The helmet's black plastic was scarred and battered from careless tossing around, but a decal of a Combat Infantryman's Badge across the forehead and the word ARMY in gold above it brightened and personalized.

Dog flicked the gas to open, snapped on his ignition, and checked to be sure he was in neutral. A touch of the start button rumbled the big Harley twin into life, and he jazzed the throttle a little to keep it running. The exhaust snapped and grumbled satisfaction, which sent the admiring boys into ecstatics.

The Harley was a 1977 FLH shovelhead, heavily customized with after-market chrome—ID number 2A11221H7. A lot of the original Harley-Davidson sheet metal had been removed from the fork and headlight area, and the stock Harley muffler baffles had been pierced to improve their sound. The rider sat low on a "Mustang" seat with a little rise to the handlebar grips.

Bikers had names for cycles like Old Dog Carlisle's. They were called putts or scooters, sometimes machines, and often simply as rides. Unlike the pampered and nearly flawless perfection of show bikes, they were used and ridden regularly.

There were riders who boasted that "Chrome don't get you home" and deliberately allowed their machines to resemble working pickup trucks. Even worse, to most eyes, were the rat bike owners, who gloried in straddling the worst looking two wheelers possible. Although their engines might hum like electric motors, rat bikers chose used stovepipe for exhausts, pop rivets for fasteners, and were sure to have folded blanket scraps for seats.

Old Dog held a thumb upright to his young audience and got an approving pair in return. His gauntleted left hand squeezed the clutch, he toed-up his kickstand, and foot tapped the shift bar down into first gear. He fed in a little throttle, eased the clutch, and almost whispered away from the curb.

He knew from a thousand other departures that the youths were studying the lines of his helmet and jacket (with the big Harley eagle stitched on) and listening to the deep thud of the customized exhaust. Hell, every biker in the world watched every other rider take off.

Valid comparisons could be made between western horsemen and Harley riders. There was something emotion-stirring about both. A man might despise horses and hate motorcycles, but still find his eyes following. Women, young women at least, were attracted to both motorcycles and horses. To explain the appeal could be difficult, but it existed, and riders so minded could be sure of feminine interest.

Old Dog swung onto Second Street and let the traffic start him north. Daytona Bike Week was coming up fast and accounted for the Harley-Davidson being on the road and tuned during the winter. One last time at Daytona? One final whooping and hollering, back-slapping, lie-swapping gathering with the rootless brothers he knew from all over the world? Yeah, Dog thought. He'd do it once more. A little different maybe, knowing this really would be a final time. He might just . . .

A jam up before the square jumbled his thoughts and he guessed he would cross the river and get out of the traffic. He leaned the bike into the left lane and found room to edge along the packed tight automobiles.

He got a look at the traffic obstruction. He should have known. Newsmen swarmed the courthouse steps and spilled into the road. An important personage was on the steps, apparently speaking into the dozen or so microphones stuck in his face. There was room on the sidewalk right in front of the speaker, and Old Dog thought he ought to swing up and roar past right under their noses. That would put him on the news, and troopers would come knocking. Beating a little traffic and annoying the honchos wasn't worth it.

A glance or two identified familiar faces. A big time trial had dominated both newspaper and nightly TV news. Probably a decision had been reached. Likely, the villain had again beaten the rap. They seemed to win with disgusting regularity.

Maybe it was vigilante time. Old Dog speculated more seriously than most would have. If the law couldn't or wouldn't remove society's obvious bad apples, wasn't it a citizen's duty to see that it got done anyway?

Apparently not, Dog had to recognize, for no one ever did anything anymore. To rise up and knock hell out of someone deserving or to seek personal vengeance or satisfaction was uncivilized and vigorously condemned. Old Dog shrugged. It wasn't his to worry about much longer. He crossed the river and turned north on 11 and 15 into Marysville. It was always a little relief to be back in Perry County. With all he had done and counting all the roads he had traveled, Perry was still home and the place he liked best.

He tried to bring Daytona Beach and Bike Week back to mind, but the irritation conjured by imagining yet another criminal beating the justice system hung on. Predators roamed and were regularly levered free of conviction by clever attorneys who sought legal loopholes and technical irregularities—never simple justice. Law and order were becoming mere catchwords.

The wise recognized that God had not decreed life would be fair, but within a society things should get better, not worse. Within this one a disgruntled minority beat, looted, and laughed. Yet a citizen who defended his livelihood was condemned, and if he dared to shoot in defense of his possessions, he was likely to be arrested and judged more harshly than the perpetrator. The law, Old Dog concluded, was not much of a criminal deterrent these days.

He was hungry, but eating usually stirred the dragon in his gut. The choices for now were to eat little bits at regular intervals and experience the hot breath only a touch more intensely or to devour a hearty, good tasting meal and suffer through the beast's fiery response.

Dog often chose the latter. Good tasting food was certainly one of life's greater pleasures. It was usually worth the exasperating, groan inducing pain it engendered.

Dog guessed he would putt up to the King's Inn, eat well, and go home to thrash through the certain discomfort. He knew how it would be. For two hours after eating he would barely sense a little heartburn. Then pain would hit. A couple of hours of abject, sweat-popping misery, followed by two more hours of gradual recovery was typical.

He wondered if he could live on milkshakes. They seldom roused the fiery monster. Probably he could survive well on them. Three months or so wasn't that long—but he would dearly miss the tasty junk food most took for granted.

Timmy Carlisle was just turning in when he heard motorcycle rumble from far across town. When the wind was right and he was tuned to it, the sound of big trucks or

Harley-Davidsons accelerating as they cleared the turn by the transmission shop caught his ear. They powered uphill, and an instant later unwound to handle the tight right turn at the new car wash. Heading north on Carlisle Street the engine rumble got lost amid buildings, but sometimes a machine gunning out of the square could be detected.

At fourteen, Tim was interested in such phenomenon. Little was more entrancing than his uncle's black and chrome Harley—unless it was Uncle Dog himself.

Yep, it was the Harley all right. To a guy who listened, every exhaust was different. Uncle Dog's had a deep, powerful growl, and when the throttle was cut back the engine gurgled like an old smoker's pipe. It was him all right.

Tim guessed he would stay up a while. To tell the truth, he was worried about his uncle. Something wasn't right, and Old Dog had been doctoring for it. He had lost weight, that was plain enough, and Tim had heard him groan out loud and swear at pain in his belly. They were all concerned. Even his mother, who didn't have much good to say about Dog Carlisle, mentioned how peaked he looked, and that it was time he got off that fool motorcycle forever.

Tim had heard the motorcycle a long way off because he had his bedroom window open. Imagine that, so warm in February that an open window felt good. He wondered if it was the greenhouse effect they studied about in school.

Uncle Dog had uncovered the Harley and rolled it onto the barn floor. Except for a little dust, it looked as sharp as when they had put it away just before Christmas. Old Dog kept his drip charger on the battery so the bike was ready to go. He did that because he might decide to take off for some strange and distant place any day. They never knew when Old Dog might say, "Guess I'll ride out and see Paul Fenske in California." An hour or two later he would be gone. Uncle Dog was exciting that way.

Uncle Dog had listened closely to a couple of weather reports, and things sounded good. With the Harley looking as anxious as they did, Old Dog had sniffed the breeze and studied the almost cloudless sky. "If I didn't know the date, I'd swear it was April."

He looked over at his nephew. "Let's check her out." Tim's nod was coolly enthusiastic, and Dog added, "Get your leathers. It'll be sharp riding."

Tim had grown. His vinyl jacket barely fit. In the fall he had worn a sweatshirt under it. Now he had trouble raising his arms. His mother would not spring for a real biker's jacket, but Old Dog had bought him a Harley insignia to sew on the vinyl. It was good enough—if you didn't really know about the right gear.

His helmet was full face, and he felt like a mummy in it, but he didn't complain. His mom was always about an inch from telling him to stay off the motorcycle. His dad wasn't likely to overrule her on Harley riding, so Timmy kept real quiet about wanting different equipment.

Uncle Dog was all leathered out and looked like a real rider—which he was if anybody ever was. Old Dog Carlisle had been riding Harleys for forty years. Forty years! Tim could hardly imagine such a time.

The stories Uncle Dog told about biking all across the country were spellbinders. If it had happened, Old Dog had been there. Sometimes, riders with beards, earrings, tattoos, and radical bikes, would show up to lay over with Old Dog for a few nights. Then the tales would be earthy, filled with swearing, and as exciting as a Rambo movie.

His father let him listen, and he knew that he and Uncle Dog had talked it over.

Dog had said, "They're salty people, Larry. Foul mouthed, blasphemous, and horrible exaggerators, but they live life to the brim. They do, see, and know things a lot of men never even hear about. Some of it's vile, but a lot more is practical knowledge a man couldn't buy or go to college for.

"Hell, Larry. I doubt there is hardly anything boys don't get a touch of by the time they're eleven or twelve. Movies don't leave much to the imagination anymore, and Playboy, Hustler, and the rest of the magazines get passed around. . . just like stuff did when we were growing up."

His dad had laughed a bit self-consciously, but he hadn't balked the way some fathers would have. His words came clear, rising from the porch where the two men sat and floating in Tim's open bedroom window.

"It's embarrassing to hear dirty talk with your son sitting there listening."

"Expect it is, but it's a hurdle you'll come up against sooner or later, Larry. It's a kind of 'You know and he knows, but everybody pretends that nobody knows' sort of thing. Tim'll handle it."

Larry Carlisle sighed, "You should have been a father, Dog. You do it better."

Old Dog stayed serious, "No, I don't do it better, and I'd make a poor father. Hell, Larry, being an uncle is easy. I can ride in, give presents, act wise, and ride out. A father's in there day in and day out, struggling with the good and the difficult. Solving another man's problems is always simple. We all figure we know more than the man doing the job. Given the chance, we would advise the president or tell the general the right way to run a war. Advice is easy, and everybody sees that hard-to-travel but just-right road other men ought to choose. Guys like me ride out of town before the going gets tough."

Old Dog had finally chuckled at his own intensity before adding, "Of course, we uncles are also good at arriving late and explaining how we'd have done it better."

A lot of the bikers that stopped by Old Dog's were hard nuts. Bearded, often ponytailed, and sometimes wearing spurs on the heels of their heavy engineer boots, they were intimidating in appearance.

Many were big men. Some were beer fatted up, but others were just large, hard, and physically capable. Only a few had the body builder's pumped and cut look. Uncle Dog claimed that a lot of riders pumped iron to build strength, but not many gave a rat's ass (his exact words) about bulging like Arnold.

Most of the visitors were one percenters—bikers who lived the rider's life style all the way. They, and their women, talked bikes, thought bikes, existed for bikes, and for little else. They knew each other, visited the same places, and among themselves spoke a biker's jargon incomprehensible to outsiders.

A bearded monster might guzzle Budweiser, belch violently while one-handing the empty into a packed aluminum disk, and say, "Puttin' into Sturgis a rice burner cut off Bat Breath's knuckler, bounced off a parked panhead, bent up his springer and front triple lacing, and wiped out the Arlen Ness scratchings on the primary cover. Bad mistake . . . "The story would continue.

Gibberish, unless the listener knew that a rice burner was a Japanese motorcycle, Bat Breath was a rider's nickname, knucklers and panheads were Harley Davidson engine types made in certain eras. Sturgis is a town in South Dakota where Harley riders swarm once a year, and Arlen Ness, a famed custom designer who, at significant expense, engraved decoration on motorcycles. Putting means riding, a springer described a front end suspension system, and triple lace denotes a custom wheel with three times the normal number of stainless or chromed spokes.

Timmy Carlisle liked knowing. Boys learn (what they want to learn) easily, and Timmy Carlisle, sitting silently off to a side, quickly mastered the biker slanguage. It was cool, very special, and often titillating with subjects his mother would have been horrified to suspect he heard or knew about.

A major discovery was that the hard-talking, outlaw-looking bikers were almost to a man gentle and reasonable behind the rough and intimidating facades. They, out of both desire and necessity, stood together against outsiders. Most were vigorously patriotic, and an astonishing percentage had served in the armed forces

As with all groups, the bikers had their ritual conformities. The leather, boots, and chained-on wallets made them instantly identifiable. Nearly all were beer guzzlers, and pot smoking was seen as acceptable behavior.

Old Dog Carlisle disapproved of the drinking and smoking. He said both were stupid and did neither himself. Tim, of course, saw it the same way.

Swearing got small attention from Dog. He gave vile language no notice—so Timmy placed no importance on knowing bad words. Old Dog helled and damned a lot, but so did nearly every man Tim knew. The best way, Tim decided, was not to use those words until you grew up, and even then you held it down around women.

The Carlisle farm—they still called it that—lay just outside Bloomfield Borough. The farmland had been sold away, and they still owned only those acres containing house, barn, an outbuilding or two, and Old Dog's shack.

Pap Carlisle had been of the old school, and in passing, he left the place to his eldest son, but when Adam Carlisle came back from the Korean Conflict he was not interested in house or land. He called his younger brother onto the porch and offered a deal.

"What I want to do, Larry, is give you the place. You and Arlis want to live here in Centre Township. You want to raise a family here. Hell, you'll want to die here. The deal will be that our old clubhouse will be mine. I'll fix it up a little and always have a place to come to."

The offer was hugely generous and was gratefully accepted. Larry and his bride of some months took over the house, and when he set up his own insurance business, Larry opened a doorway into a side bedroom and created an office.

The clubhouse was a former chicken coop the boys had cleaned out and appropriately decorated. Old Dog had made a project out of insulating, illegally attaching a bathroom to the house septic system, and adding a broad porch for sitting. Later, he nailed on a carport which sheltered motorcycles and his ratty-looking pickup that ran like a watch.

Dog's furnishings had been upgraded to yard sale quality, but the aging boyish posters and drawings still hung about the walls. While Old Dog was away, Larry punched a hole in a wall and hung on a heat pump. Dog still had the pot bellied stove if he wanted it, but the heat pump also provided air conditioning. Dog was appreciative and said so.

Chapter 5

When the Harley grumbled up the drive and dropped into idle at Dog's shack, Larry Carlisle put down his paper and waited. He would give Old Dog time to get his jacket off and drain tanks before he went over.

The motorcycle idled, barely chugging, repeating a comforting "potato, potato, potato." Tuned just right, Larry thought. He grinned to himself. An older Harley Davidson should idle higher. The engine starved for oil at slow idle. Dog knew that, of course, and damn, it did sound good.

Arlis asked, "Why doesn't he turn that thing off? He always sits there letting it run on. That engine makes the TV jump." It didn't, of course, but Larry did not argue about it

They sat in their personal chairs, almost turned away from each other. Larry sometimes wondered if there was symbolism there. Arlis could be shrewish a bit too often lately.

Actually, the seating was arranged so that Arlis could watch the tube while he read without the thing catching his eye. When he watched TV, it took only a little shifting and propping to see just fine. They had watched *Matlock* together until it was cancelled, and they usually made a point of seeing the special mini-series programs. Larry watched the evening news and on Sunday saw David Brinkley while Arlis was still in church. They had it pretty well worked out . . . about like they had routinized the rest of their lives, he supposed.

Not much excitement hit Bloomfield. Like everyone else, they shopped the new Food Rite on the same night of each week and listened distantly to the Carson Long military school drum corps sounding off every Saturday morning. The fact was, they both liked life just as it was, no big surprises—good or bad—comfortable and secure.

Their son, Timmy, was just breaking into high school sports, and they looked forward to that excitement. Parents followed athletics closely while they had boys or girls on the teams. A year or two before and afterward, they rarely knew who won or lost. The Larry Carlisles would be the same.

Old Dog was the family wild card. He blew in, sometimes like a cyclone, occasionally merely a zephyr that barely ruffled tranquility. That was part of Old Dog's attraction. You never knew what might happen.

Once motorcycles bellowed like wounded steers along Main Street, and people rushed to their doors to see. Nearly fifty riders muscled their machines through town and into the Carlisle yard. For an hour Old Dog hosted with beer, soft drinks, and food before the mob saddled up and thundered back through the village.

During the invasion, the Carlisle phone had run continuously and Arlis was afraid to go outside. A state trooper made a few slow passes, but the crowd appeared friendly. Timmy was glued to his Uncle Dog's hip, a small fist clutching Dog's chap belt, his eyes like saucers, hanging on every scent and sound. Larry circulated, finding handshakes without challenge and a lot of pleasant feeling beneath the chains and leather. He could be sure of a laugh by offering insurance coverage if the applicant would sell his bike. Larry enjoyed it.

Another night, Old Dog had ridden in slow. It was not particularly late, but they heard the Harley fall over, and Dog's steps were stumbly on his porch. He fumbled around his door and Arlis had said, "He's drunk!"

Old Dog did not drink. As far as Larry knew, he never had. He heard Timmy soft footing across the porch roof. The boy would slide down a corner post onto the porch. He often went out that way when his uncle came home. Larry usually heard him, but he did not think Arlis had ever worked out the creaking of the tin roof under her son's careful steps. Getting back wasn't as easy for Tim. He had to labor up the rose trellis, avoiding all the thorns. Usually, he chanced the squeaky, give-away stairs coming in.

Larry let Tim get there first. The boy stood over the fallen Harley. Wordlessly they hoisted it upright and Timmy toed down the kickstand to support it. The ignition was still on, and Tim snapped it off and shut off the gas line.

Old Dog slumped against his table edge, head hanging, striving with fumbling fingers to remove his jacket. When he looked up, his features were swollen and bloody. Larry heard his son's gasp.

While they cleaned him up, they got Old Dog's story. The explanation was shorter than the cleanup, but Dog drew it out, apologizing for causing so much trouble. They were taking so much time that Arlis arrived to investigate. She took charge and things went faster.

Dog had been pounded hard. His nose was bent, he was cut deep under an eye, and both lips had been split. Something solid had raised knots on his head, big lumps, each of which must have dazed; head knocking with a leather wrapped sap they learned. Not hard enough blows to fracture a skull, but dazing, painful, ugly cracks that were supposed to teach lessons and leave messages.

Dog's body had also been worked over. Dog expected nothing had broken, but. . . he grinned raggedly . . . "They sure loosened some glue joints."

Old Dog's knuckles were skinned, so he had gotten in some licks, but his shins were scraped raw where heavy boots had been rasped along them. The men who had laid on the beating clearly knew their business.

Dog had come onto a brother being kicked into a pulp by three men. A brother meant someone in biker garb, known or a stranger. It did not matter.

Old Dog had jumped in, but the brother was already far gone, and another thug had been waiting in their car. The brother went down to stay, and Dog had all four to himself.

Their beating had been generally impersonal. It was what they did for a living. They pinned Dog against a wall and held him while they worked.

The head knocker had said, "Don't ever interfere in Bat Stailey's business. That clear?" Dog had not answered fast enough, and that was when a big fist had cut his eye, split his lips, and busted his nose.

He had tried kicking. That was resented, and one or more had ripped him from the knee down with the edge of his shoe sole. That had really hurt, and Dog was thankful for his jump boots that cushioned some of it.

Old Dog had his five-shot derringer in a jacket pocket, but it might as well have been at home; he couldn't get to it. By the time they let him go, he didn't have enough left to try.

The brother came to first, and they helped each other erect. Dog got astride, the Harley started, and the brother went off somewhere. Cool air rushing by had woken Dog up a little, and he had made it home.

Arlis said, "You should have gone straight to the hospital."

"You're right, but it's OK now."

"It's not OK. You could have serious damage inside your head."

Timmy's voice was shrill with tension. "Where was your helmet, Uncle Dog? It should have helped."

Old Dog looked confused. "Don't know, Tim. It was on when I started. Fastened tight, too, but I didn't have it on riding home. Glad I didn't. Wind blowing through kept me going.

Larry was practical. "It wouldn't have fit over these lumps, Adam. Whew, this one split the skin a little."

Arlis shooed him away and dabbed at the wound with a warm, wet cloth.

Tim had popped outside and came back holding Old Dog's helmet. "It was laying off to the side, Uncle Dog. Fell off when the bike went down."

"The bike went down?"

Larry reassured. "It's all right. We got it up. No damage."

"You didn't even turn off the ignition, Uncle Dog. You just hit the kill button and got off."

"I'll be damned! I thought I was moving smooth and acting smart."

Tim said, "Your helmet strap's been sliced, Uncle Dog." He held the shell out for examining.

"He's right, Dog. Sliced clean, like a razor would cut." Larry felt himself shudder a little.

"This is serious, Dog. Those guys weren't just fooling around."

From his bed, Old Dog snorted. "You just discovering that, Larry? I got the idea about the time that fourth guy got out of the car.

"But like they said, it wasn't personal. I was just being convinced not to mess in Bat Stailey's manure pile. Hell, one of 'em must have hung the helmet over the backrest. They figured they were being kind."

Dog thought aloud. "I wonder how come I didn't feel that helmet coming off during the fight." He groaned and shifted in discomfort.

"Because you were already punched numb. You're lucky they didn't cut your throat."

Tim said, "Your helmet isn't ruined, Uncle Dog. There's enough strap left to sew back together."

Old Dog's answer was a little distant, as though relaxing was drifting him into sleep.

Arlis considered, "When patients have head injuries they don't like to give them medications. It confuses symptoms."

Timmy was admiring, "Wow, Mom, you know things."

His mother turned on him. "I know you should be in bed. Get! "

Then kinder, "We'll be right along."

Tim said, "Be sure Uncle Dog's got the horn ready, Mom." He went as told. He and Old Dog had an understanding about not hanging back and acting whiny.

The horn was a boater's compressed gas warning signal. Press the button, and it uttered a piercing wail that set teeth on edge but alerted drawbridge tenders. They had gotten it during a broken leg time, when they had feared Old Dog might need sudden help. He hadn't, but the horn had been a good idea.

Larry found it on a shelf and placed it by the bed. "Blow if your head feels bad, Dog. Don't wait to see if it goes away. Arlis is right. Head injuries can turn bad suddenly."

Dog said, "Thanks, brother. I'll sleep, and by morning I'll feel better."

"Like hell you will. You'll be worse. For the next few days you are going to be one sorry mess."

Larry started out. He hit the light switch, and through the dark heard his brother's voice.

"Does my insurance cover this, Larry? You sure sold me enough of it."

"Only if you go to a doctor, Dog."

Larry stepped out, then leaned back inside.

"Tell you what, Adam, you sell that motorcycle, and I'll get you some real coverage."

Old Dog did not bother to answer.

That had been two years ago. Dog had healed swiftly. Once in a while he mentioned Bat Stailey, but like the hired thugs, Old Dog seemed to consider the battering impersonal and something to overlook and move on.

Timmy had asked, "Who's Bat Stailey?"

"A very bad man, son." Larry had not been specific; Stailey was said to be in prostitution, gambling, loan sharking, and protection. It was always "said to be." No one proved anything. Stailey's heavy hand was known to be on many things, but he left no prints. Stailey had endured two flashy, media-show trials and won both. Everyone knew what he was, but no one delivered the proof.

Stailey was listed in the yellow pages as a used furniture dealer. Al Capone had claimed the same.

Chapter 6

Larry Carlisle wished this walk to Dog's shack held nothing more serious than discovery of a physical beating, but he knew better.

In his explanation, Old Dog had not danced around. His still wiry body was riddled with cancer. It was in his bones, his lungs, and his liver. The cancer was in his stomach. Lymph nodes were giving up. They swelled and pained like fire. A few had been surgically removed. A couple were neutralized by radiation. The filters were effectively gone.

Doc Klein had brought in the most expert. Old Dog had held no particular hope, but he had gone down for a final, final word. His brother expected he knew what the report had been.

Larry heard Dog's toilet flush, and he clumped a little on the porch so his brother would know he was there. Dog came in a minute, taking a long pull on an aqua colored Mylanta bottle. He sank into one of his old porch rockers and massaged his stomach. "Geez, my gut's on fire."

Before Larry could comment, perhaps embarrassed by complaining, Dog quickly added, "What a night this is! Imagine, sitting on the front porch in February."

"Changing tonight." Larry postponed what he had come to hear. He parroted the Channel 27 weatherman. "A cold arctic air mass is sweeping in from the northwest and will drop our local temperatures into the low teens by late tonight. The Alberta Express is coming folks, and by the weekend we can expect freezing conditions."

"Daytona's only a long week away. I'll be down in the sun thinking of you freezing up here."

"You're going to Daytona, Dog?"

"Yep, assuming everything holds together."

They rocked a little before Larry came to the point of his visit.

"What did Doc Klein say, Adam?"

Dog's reply was measured, avoiding irony or attempting false lightheartedness.

"He said nothing had changed and that heavy treatment wasn't worth going through." Dog's voice flattened. "He recommended pain control—nothing more.

"The various doctors decided that I was doing remarkably well for the advanced condition I'm in." Old Dog allowed a small chuckle. "Which I took to mean that I ought to hurt a lot worse than I do.

"And," Dog cleared his throat to make the words clear. "Doc said I might have three months on my feet, but it could be less."

"Oh hell, Adam." Just ninety days; Larry was stunned by the immediacy.

Dog speculated aloud. "You know, that three months stuff bothers me. Sounds like a bad movie script. Why not four months, or maybe two and a half months? It's always, 'You have three months to live.'"

Tim came trotting across the yard.

"Hi, Uncle Dog."

His father said, "I thought you went to bed."

"I heard the Harley, and I wanted to tell Uncle Dog about my workout."

"Make it short, son. We've business to talk over."

"How'd it go, Tim? Have a good one?"

"Yeah, real good. I could feel my muscles pump."

"Uh huh."

"I skipped rope for three rounds and punched the heavy bag, too." Tim saw Old Dog rubbing his belly the way he did when it hurt.

"Sounds good, Tim. You're getting in three workouts a week, and that's just right." Dog searched for a point or two to emphasize. The boy was sticking to it, and training now would pay off in high school ball. God, his stomach burned. No more meals!

"Don't overdue the pumping when you are lifting weights. Pumping makes a muscle big but not a lot stronger. Body builders pump up. Power lifters just get stronger. Keep your hands high when you are hitting the bags. Guys get to hammering away, and their fists get down by their waists. They're wide open. A bag won't punch back, but a man will. Defense counts.

Keep the fist not hitting up high, protecting your face."

"I'm working on that, Uncle Dog." Tim squared off and stabbed at the air, shadowboxing an imaginary opponent.

"Looks good. Nice body shift Step left and right Give 'em angles. Makes you harder to hit."

Larry said, "I can remember you practicing that when we were kids. When I tried I sprained my wrist hitting the big bag."

"You did all right, brother. You were first string in football and baseball."

Larry laughed more than a little self-consciously. "You know damned well that Bloomfield High was so small that unless we all played we couldn't field a team. You were the jock in our family, Dog."

Old Dog turned back to the boy. "You remember Harvey Thebes, who shot one thousand points in basketball a few years ago?"

"Course I remember him, Uncle Dog. He lives up the road. I see him almost every day."

"Well, fame passes quickly, and I wasn't so sure you'd remember. Anyway, Harv shot three hundred baskets a day all through high school. That means in the rain, and he scraped the snow away to shoot in the winter.

"That's how an athlete gets good. He trains harder. Every day that you work out in the bam inches you ahead. However far you go in sports will be a hint further because of today's workout. Put a hundred workouts together and you can measure the gain. Imagine what a thousand can do."

The father said, "Enough, coach."

He turned to his son. "Call it a night, Tim. Your uncle and I want to talk."

"Yeah but . . ." Tim remembered. "Good night, Dad; good night, Uncle Dog." He trotted away, dribbling and shooting an imaginary basketball.

Old Dog's sigh was deep. "I wish I could see how he'll turn out."

The brother's voice choked a little. "Well, maybe you will see, Adam. We don't know for sure what happens in heaven."

Dog lightened the mood. "Expect all I'll see are the soles of shoes, Larry. I haven't been that good an example."

"You have for Tim, Adam. He dotes on you." It was the brother's turn to sigh. "We've got to tell him pretty soon, Dog. He knows you aren't well. Asked me about it a week ago. I hedged around, but we ought to square up with what's happening.

"Yep, and it's my job, seeing I'm the one doing the dying. I don't want any more of this rubbing off on you than it has to, Larry. I'll make it as easy for both of us as I can."

"God, Dog, I'm not worrying about myself, or Arlis, or Tim for that matter. It's you I hurt for."

Old Dog was uncomfortable with the weight of the talk.

"Tell you what, brother, there's one thing you can do for me that I'd really feel good about"

"Name it, Dog."

Old Dog hesitated only an organizing instant

"I'm feeling decent, and I'm going to Daytona Beach Bike Week to see and do one last time.

"Fact is, I'd like to take Timmy down with me to see the bikes and the people. I'd like to show him a last good time that he'll remember all of his life."

Dog sounded rueful. "That isn't a great monument to leave, but I'd really like doing it."

Larry blew softly. "God, Arlis will kill me."

Old Dog waited him out

"You know, Dog, when I was Tim's age I'd have given anything for a trip like you're proposing, but Pap would have said, 'No,' and that would have ended it.

"Why not? Why shouldn't I say 'Yes?' I wouldn't want my son growing old remembering that his Dad had said, 'No' simply because it was safest and easiest."

"Accidents can happen, Larry."

"I know, Adam, and don't argue against yourself.

"We didn't have Timmy, Arlis and me, until it was almost too late, and we have thanked the Lord a million times for allowing us a son. Tim coming late makes us kind of over-protective some times and timid about normal boy things that younger parents don't think much about. When Timmy swings on a grapevine I get nervous. I let you teach him to shoot because I was afraid I'd do it poorly or incomplete somehow."

Dog interrupted. "Hell, Larry, you're at least as good a shot as I am. You hunt every season. I don't hardly go out anymore. You could've . . ."

Larry went on as though unhearing. "Arlis is scared to death of your motorcycle. When Timmy goes with you, I can see her jaw muscles work straining to keep silent." He groaned in exasperation.

"I've played it safe my whole life, and I'm not complaining about how things are turning out. So far I think we've done well, but it's just as true that smothering a son isn't right, either."

Larry's mood shifted and excitement tinged his voice. "Remember our first plane ride, Dog? Old John Buck took us up."

"Yeah, we thought he could fly like the Red Baron or at least like Charles Lindbergh."

"God, Bloomfield Airport's a cart track now. Anyway, Pap had a conniption fit when he heard. Never let us go up again with Mister Buck or Clair Raffensburger or any of the pilots."

"They were good flyers, Larry."

"That's my point, Adam. Pap let his fears for us rule his head. We missed some experiences that might have opened other tracks and interests. Who knows what we lost out on."

"Somebody, maybe it was old Will Rogers, wrote, 'I never regretted anything I did, only the things I didn't do.'"

"That's it, Dog, and you have lived pretty close to that saying."

"Well, if I have, I've taken a lot of knocks doing it, and Will Rogers, if it was him that said it, died in a plane crash up in Alaska."

"Do you think it's dangerous taking Timmy to Daytona, Adam?"

Old Dog swigged again at his Mylanta. He said, "I'm going to try Riopan Plus; this stuff's lost its wallop."

He answered his brother with care. "Maybe two hundred thousand motorcycles will be coming to Daytona. Some will be there for hell raising, but not all. The record is that no one gets killed. A few bones get broken and a lot of unreported chrome gets scraped.

"No, it isn't dangerous. It's loud and it's carefree. Too many drink too much beer, but I don't. Some get reckless, but not the guys I visit with. Mostly we talk, ride the beach, look at bikes, and watch the races. We go to the swap meet and visit the Harley display. If you act right, the week is about as dangerous as the Bloomfield or Newport Firemen's Carnival."

Larry laughed, "That isn't too dangerous, Dog."

"No, it isn't. Daytona is adventurous because it is big and different, that's all."

They rocked a little before Larry said, "OK, Adam. A week out of school won't hurt. Hell, Tim will learn a thousand times more traveling with you than he would in school anyway.

"OK, if his mother doesn't threaten to leave or something, he can go. When is it, anyway?"

"Second week in March we'll be there."

"Whew, that is close."

"It better be. After that I plan on getting my ducks in line, if you know what I mean."

"Yeah, guess I do, Adam. You sure you want Tim to go along . . . this last time?"

"One hundred percent sure. I've things to show and tell, brother."

Old Dog's mind seemed to wander, as though he were examining something important.

"I'm considering taking on a sort of personal project, Larry. Sort of clean up a mess that no one seems willing to tackle." He mused again. "Could be I've got a special opportunity here. Maybe it's a calling I can use to mean something."

Dog shook himself into the present. "Anyway, if I go ahead with what I'm considering, it won't take long, maybe a week or two."

Larry wondered what in hell Dog could be referring to. He supposed Adam would tell him in time. Then Old Dog delivered a stunner.

"I'm aiming to check out of here by May first, brother. I've never hedged about having a dying plan. It looks as if I'll have the opportunity to do what I've always said I wanted to do."

"Aw, Dog, you don't have to . . ."

"I know I don't have to, Larry. You've got to understand that I want to, and part of it is not waiting too long. Doc Klein's going to fix me up, so even that is coming easy."

"You're going to Alaska?"

"That's how I've described it since I decided back in . . . when was it? Middle 50s, I guess."

Larry Carlisle rocked in silence, admiring his brother, maybe more than he ever had, saddened almost to illness by the inevitability of Old Dog's death, but proud of his brother's will to do it on his own terms—really on his own terms, just as he had said he would for about the last forty years.

No one listened much when Old Dog brought up dignified dying. Self-deliverance, he called it, and getting out of the way when you became a burden was part of his description. His personal plan was heard then ignored, as if Old Dog had rambled on about what he would do if he were president.

But Larry Carlisle had always believed Adam was serious, and if fate dealt the right hand, Old Dog Carlisle would pass on the way he chose and where he chose. When, had always been the game's question, but it appeared life's lottery had even popped that date into view. May Day, an old pagan and Druid ceremonial date.

Chapter 7

Arlis barely held off the emotional fit her husband expected. She managed because . . . because she knew she had been acting short tempered and shrewish recently and because Larry Carlisle really did want Timmy to go off on a stupid trip with his uncle.

First Arlis complained about missed school days, but she knew as well as anyone that grades did not crash because of flu or suspension or due to particular team or club absences. They would not because of Daytona Bike Week. Of course she groused about the dangers of motorcycle riding, but Timmy already rode behind Old Dog so often that the argument lacked impact.

When her husband was earnest about something, Arlis listened. Larry Carlisle was a comfortable man, like a favorite shoe, and he deserved respect and consideration. He had stayed true and dependable, just as she had known he would back in high school days.

Larry's business had prospered, and the Carlisles were reasonably secure. Arlis recognized herself as better situated than most who showed up for class reunions.

There was a final detail that also influenced her grudging acceptance of their son's adventure. Knowingly or otherwise, the former Arlis Doyle loved Larry Carlisle and preferred to please him. She wished often that she could cast out the devils of spite and envy that popped so often to her too ready tongue. Arlis prayed fervently each Sunday for help in being less testy, tart, and outspoken.

If prayers helped, Arlis Carlisle did not care to visualize what she would be like without them. Having the failings was bad enough, being acutely aware of them was worse. Arlis was prone to a little faith in astrology. She was a Sagittarius, and they were known for being sharp tongued and bitingly forthright. Perhaps it was all in her stars, and her best efforts never could help.

The problem was Old Dog. He had always been a thorn. Well, not always . . . she could confess that only to herself, and only during special moments.

She was two years younger than Dog Carlisle, the 1949-1950 crush of half the girls in Bloomfield High. Dog had a certain untamed manner that just demanded capture and pacifying by a fortunate Bloomfield beauty. That senior year, Adam Carlisle's name swam through many passionate female fantasies. The competition was severe, and although no special girl seemed to win the hero's heart for more than a few days, a hopeful sophomore like Arlis Doyle (whose first name was—surely cosmically—present as the very center of Adam Carlisle's last name) had little chance.

Arlis did manage a private Coke date at Book's Drug Store, but despite her best eye batting and intense interest in every Carlisle vowel, Dog moved on without a backward glance. He starred in three sports, and against Newport he slammed a home run so powerful the ball landed on the roof of the high school building. Adam Carlisle truly fluttered girlish hearts.

Larry Carlisle played in his brother's shadow. "Good player, Larry, but old Dog was the kind of athlete I like to watch."

Unlike his older brother, Larry paid attention to Arlis Doyle. They were classmates, and it was clear to any evaluating eye that Larry would be a steady, stay at home kind of man who would work hard providing for his family.

Larry looked like a good catch. The Carlisle's property had a nice older home, and the father was known to be slowly dying, peacefully following an only half remembered wife and mother, gone many, many years.

Larry did not pluck heart strings the way Dog did, but Adam was gone off to war and might never return. Out of sight could be out of mind. Arlis applied herself, and Larry Carlisle fell like an overripe peach. They were married shortly after graduation and took up housekeeping in Larry's old room.

Pap Carlisle went to his reward about on schedule and was duly interred beside his wife in Bloomfield cemetery. Then . . . Adam reappeared in Valley Forge Army Hospital, wounded in the fighting, but expected to recover.

Pap Carlisle's will had stunned Arlis. She had never suspected that everything would go to Adam. It just wasn't done that way anymore. Larry was struggling to become an insurance man, and the rewards were small. Arlis really could not imagine herself living in the same home with Adam, and whomever he ended up marrying. She and Larry would be out, and her expected comfortable security would be gone.

Dog came home a few times, his left arm strapped to his chest. Korean War soldiers were not welcomed home as enthusiastically as World War Two warriors had been, but Dog did not appear to care. He made obligatory rounds and slept in his own room. He ate with his brother and his almost new wife, telling a few funny war stories, but avoiding discussion of when he would come home to stay and what would happen then.

Arlis jabbed at her husband to speak up and find out if Dog was throwing them into the street. She wanted to know. Arlis just expected she was going to end up waitressing or working in a dress factory instead of keeping house, the way she wished to. She wanted Larry to ask for half of what Pap Carlisle had left, but she wisely kept that counsel. If they got put out, then she would speak out herself.

Dog got well. He was stationed at Fort Meade, but would not be in the Army much longer. Larry was openly proud of his First Lieutenant brother, wounded and decorated serving his country. Larry Carlisle was his own man and did not feel lessened by Adam's accomplishments—but Arlis did.

Flashy Adam, wearing all his fancy ribbons, strutting around the county, just wallowing in all the admiration simply made Arlis' blood boil. In her mind it made Larry and their steady living appear dull and hicky—like anything they did or got couldn't hold a candle to Adam the hero who had been everywhere and done everything.

Arlis would have been appalled if a friend had suggested that she was jealous of Dog's attention-catching charisma, and that she should forget her girlish crush on Dog and be grateful for the solid, hardworking man she had. None did, because Arlis limited most of her fuming to her secret thoughts and appeared to everyone as mildly disinterested in her brother-in-law's successes.

The facts were, Lieutenant Dog Carlisle rarely wore his uniform off-post He did not seek audiences and did not join veterans' organizations or parade in the Memorial Day activities. Dog kept mostly to himself. He roamed the woods some, with Larry's young farm hound for company, and he worked out with the weights and punching bags he and Larry had left in the barn.

For his part, Larry Carlisle preferred to wait and see. When Adam wanted the house, he and Arlis would move out. What was tough about that? Most couples started from scratch, and they had already enjoyed a rent-free year or so.

It was natural to feel that Pap should have divided up what he had, but their father had been a close Bible student, and some of the ancient beliefs had gripped him. Everything to the first son had turned out to be one of them. Of course, biblically speaking, the inheriting son was then to provide for his siblings. Larry could not see how Dog could do much of that. Dog, after all, would soon be unemployed and job hunting. He would have enough difficulty taking care of himself.

Dog supposed he was going through some sort of readjustment problem. It wasn't that the war loomed in his memory or haunted midnight sweats. It was that little interested him. His attention span was distressingly short. He grew swiftly bored with conversation, after a few pages his mind drifted, and he read and reread books, magazines, and newspapers without comprehension.

He wanted to be out of the army, and they would let him go soon, but thoughts of job seeking ... with all the appropriate humilities and humbling perseverance thereafter was tortuous.

The military did offer a perverse sort of freedom absent in civilian life. In the army, no one knew or cared what you did off-duty—providing you never brought reportable discredit to the service. Just be on time, in uniform, "bright eyed and bushy tailed," and no questions were raised. A soldier could race cars, chase women, drink himself stupid and bay at the moon—no one cared. Just be on the job when you were scheduled.

Freedom held appeal, but Dog could not see a lifetime of Left, Face; Forward, March. Military regimentation countered any off-duty privileges, and the army was going to dump him anyway. It was swamped with young officers. To stay, Lieutenant Carlisle would have to attend college and touch a lot of career bases. Jump school and Ranger training were tempting, but rotten duty tours, like Korea again, were not.

Dog wanted out, but to what he was not sure.

Sergeant Bailey had a motorcycle. At quitting time the sergeant straddled his machine, got a good grip on the handlebars and backed into the street. He kick started, twice with the ignition off and the choke on, then a third powerful kick with the ignition on, the spark in his left hand retarded, and invariably the engine belched bluish smoke and started. Bailey revved a few times, heeled the clutch and left handed his tank-mounted gearshift into first. His boot toe eased the rocker-like clutch into gear, and the bike moved away as smooth as a stone sliding on ice.

Lieutenant Carlisle was fascinated. Almost daily he observed the procedure and watched the sergeant lean his motorcycle around a turn and on out of sight. The rap of the engine could be heard for a long time.

There had always been motorcycles around, but Dog had never paid attention to them. If he thought at all about motorcycles, it was that they were probably fun to ride, but they were also dangerous, noisy, and useless in bad weather. He assumed most people felt the same.

Yet, watching Bailey move out kept catching his interest. There was appeal in the control of a powerful machine, and there appeared to be a kind of personal freedom riding in the wind astride such a responsive iron monster. Dog saw a comparison with riding a horse—the way a westerner did—solid in the saddle with places to go.

He said, "I like your motorcycle, Sergeant."

"Thank you, sir. Are you a rider?"

"Nope, don't know a thing about them, but I'd like to know more."

"What can I tell you, Lieutenant? There's nothing mysterious about them."

"Are they hard to ride? You make it look easy enough."

The sergeant chuckled. "If you can ride a bicycle, learning takes about fifteen minutes. I'm not saying that would make you much of a rider, but from then on it's just practice."

"That easy?"

Sergeant Bailey was willing to help out. "Pile on, Lieutenant, and I'll show you how."

Dog watched as Bailey snapped an extra supporting spring into place underneath the long buddy seat. "Got to have that to carry double, Lieutenant."

The sergeant straddled his machine and revved the engine until it warmed and smoothed.

"OK, Lieutenant, climb on." He pointed to a pair of protruding pipes just behind his own foot pads. "Put your feet there, and don't take 'em off. I'll do all the bike supporting. Around corners just lean into the curve a little, like you would on a bicycle—nothing to it."

Even Sergeant Bailey's gentle acceleration was startling, and it snapped Dog's head and body backward so that he grabbed quickly at Bailey's leather jacket to hold on. The sergeant hollered over his shoulder, "You'll get used to it fast. Everybody does."

They cruised across the army post onto back roads where little traffic appeared. Bailey explained the motorcycle's operation.

"OK, reach around me." The sergeant slid forward onto the motorcycle's gas tanks to give more room.

"Your right hand is on the throttle. Twist it in and you'll go faster." Dog did, and the engine rumble became a deeper bellow. Speed picked up.

Bailey said, "Your left hand controls the spark. It stays on, which is all the way in, except when you are starting the engine. Then you retard it by turning out. If you don't retard, your engine will probably kickback, and that will hurt. It can sprain an ankle or even break one. That's why when we kick over we come down on the pedal full force. Boy, you don't want kickbacks."

Bailey was right. Handling the motorcycle felt easy. Dog operated the gearshift while Bailey managed the foot clutch. They leaned like one through turns, accelerating out of them with what Dog felt was sparkling power. He got off in front of his office reluctantly.

"Damn, Sergeant, that is pure fun."

"Thought you liked it, Lieutenant"

Dog nodded, "I think I'll get one."

Bailey's interest sharpened. "I can make you a good offer on this machine, if you mean it, Lieutenant. I've got orders to Germany, and I plan on shipping my car. Can't take 'em both over."

"Hell, I don't know enough about them yet, Bailey."

"Well, I can tell you what I know, and I'll give you a handful of *Enthusiast* magazines. That's Harley-Davidson's publication. Tells all about Harley riding.

"If you're interested, I'll make the price right, but I need the bike for a week or so."

Dog began learning. There were two American companies making motorcycles, and a number of English models were popular. Harley-Davidson and Indian were in competition, but it seemed clear that in the Maryland area, Harley had the popularity.

Dog borrowed Bailey's cycle for practice. Riding was easy, but real control was not. As long as no difficulties arose, anyone could wheel down the road, but if something went wrong, handling a motorcycle could be a sudden and violently dangerous emergency.

Bailey's Harley was a 1947, 45 cubic inch flathead. It was a pretty machine with some chrome accessories, but it was not the latest model and was the least powerful of Harley designs. Dog found the local Harley shop and dropped in to talk motorcycles.

The owner, salesman, and chief mechanic was Monty. Harleys were his life. Monty's wedding had included a one hundred bike escort, and the honeymooners left town on a 1949 hydra-glide, 74 overhead.

Of course, Monty wished to sell Dog a new machine, but he did not push too hard. "Bailey's bike is all right to learn on. Hell, I sold it to him. If you buy it, I'll take it in trade when you move up.

"And you will move up, Dog." They stuck to nicknames.

"About the third Triumph or Indian that leaves you sitting will get you interested in more power."

Dog suspected Monty was right, but Dog tried to invest wisely, and money came hard. Bailey would sell for two hundred dollars. A new 74 came close to one thousand dollars.

Monty said, "Bailey's flathead will do about eighty miles per hour. That will sound fast until some grandpa dusts you off with his Buick Roadmaster. A 74 will go like hell and top out over one hundred. If you ride a lot, you'll get to wanting one."

Dog doubted he would care about the top speed. God, one hundred miles an hour on two wheels was frightening even to think about.

The dealer went on. "The worst thing about a forty-five is that they are puny carrying two people. The engine just isn't up to hauling double the way most guys want to ride."

Dog had already begun to feel that. The acceleration that had at first seemed so remarkable was quickly mastered, and he felt the weak response when he opened the throttle.

Dog read all the literature. Harleys were around in 45 flatheads and 74-cubic-inch knuckle and panheads. Probably there were others. There were also 61-inch and 80-cubic-inch flatheads. Learning the strengths and weaknesses was tasty, and the photographs of pilot-capped riders in boots and britches cruising pastoral byways could be entrancing.

Lieutenant Dog Carlisle bought Sergeant Bailey's flathead Harley. He rode it hard locally and back and forth to Pennsylvania. The military was probably a trifle uncertain about commissioned officers tooling motorcycles around the post, but Lieutenant Carlisle was about out anyway.

Before the leaves turned, Dog Carlisle traded his forty-five to Monty's cycle shop for a new, dark blue seventy-four overhead. The new Harley had a chrome fork and handlebars. There were three chrome headlights, and the buddy seat sported a dressy chrome bar for hanging on to.

On his day of discharge, Dog filled his leather saddle bags and strapped a half filled duffel bag across the back fender. Everything else had already been ferried to Bloomfield. He stopped for a handshake with Monty and headed north. In three hours he was home in Perry County.

A short note, sent to all customers from Monty's cycle shop reached Dog a week later. While road testing a repaired cycle, Monty had been crushed under a truck making a sudden and un-signaled left turn.

The motorcycle shop was closing down.

Chapter 8

Going to Daytona took some preparation. In years past, Old Dog had done most of it himself. This time he took the pickup down to Jim Tressler for an oil change and greasing. He oversaw Timmy's work on the Harley. Mostly it was polishing because they wished to look good, but the oil bag was down a little, and Old Dog wanted the chain taken up just a turn. Of course, they put in a new rear spark plug. That happened about every third tank of gas.

Old Dog had a nifty bike lift for lots of jobs—including polishing and cleaning. Tim could slide the lift underneath the motorcycle and hand pump or put compressor air to it, and the big Harley rose about eighteen inches where it was handy to work on.

Of course, adjusting chain tension was done with the bike solid on its wheels. Off the ground, tensions changed and adjustments would not be right when weight again rested on its wheels.

Adjusting the chain was not difficult. It was a matter of loosening two big nuts before turning a pair of bolts that moved the back wheel exactly the same amount, then checking that the wheel still ran true before tightening down again.

"The new Harley belt drives need even less adjusting, Tim. They're the way to go, but old riders stick with the stuff they're familiar with.

"Hell, the Harley Twin V engine is something like seventy years old. The new Evolution engine is just an improved model, but damned good upgrading, I've got to admit."

"Why don't you have an Evolution, Uncle Dog?"

Old Dog scrubbed across his forehead, as if searching for passable reasons.

"Well, to my eyes an 'Evo' looks like something out of Japan. There's a look missing. Can't exactly put words to it.

"It sounds dumb, but there isn't much work a man can do on an Evolution. Belt drives and electronic ignitions work better than the old stuff. Gets to be like driving a car. You push a few buttons and away you go. Where's the old spirit of adventure? What happened to the challenge?"

Old Dog snorted a little at his own reasonings. "Of course, even older riders claimed the same thing when electric start came along. Claimed that if you didn't kick 'em, they weren't real motorcycles.

"Some were still claiming that about springer forks when I started in the early 1950s. If you didn't have coil springs showing behind your headlight, your ride wasn't the real thing."

"Springers are coming back now, Uncle Dog. There are some beauties in the new *Easyriders*."

"You been into my magazines again? You're just reading them to study all the naked women posing on show bikes. I think I'll tell your mother."

"I am not." Tim was indignant. "Sometimes I even wish they weren't there, so I could see the motorcycles better."

"I do myself . . . sometimes. You'll see lots of those biking ladies in Daytona, Tim. Most aren't all that gorgeous, but the cycles are. Beautiful machines down there."

Old Dog backed the pickup against a bank, and Tim put across an eight-foot-long steel ramp. Dog eased the

Old Dog

Harley up slow, getting lined up, then drove along the ramp and into the truck bed.

When he shut down, Tim said, "Whew, I get nervous every time you do that, Uncle Dog. Falling off that ramp would be awful."

"Surely would. Nose Nagle, a friend of mine, was loading a rice burner at Precision Cycle down in Sarasota. Stalled and went off sideways. Nose couldn't get clear. No crash bars, of course, so after the engine snapped his leg, it cooked him more than a little. Smelled terrible."

Timmy said, "Wow!"

"Yep. Nose never rode a Jap bike again. Sticks to American iron like he ought to."

The Harley was tied down and covered well, so it would shine when they got to Florida. Their duffel was stuffed into sail bags, and the bags went into footlockers to stay clean and dry.

They were ready.

It was raining and biting cold when they drove out of Bloomfield. Good weather to leave behind, Old Dog claimed.

Their start was late. Timmy's mother had a lot of last minute warnings, and his Dad laid on a few more about doing just what Uncle Dog told him and to be careful. Tim thought they would never get done.

Uncle Dog was slow himself and looked as though he hadn't slept too well, but he climbed behind the wheel, pointed a pistol finger at his brother in some sort of shared meaning, and suggested Arlis quit worrying; they were going to have fun.

They passed a loaded school bus going through Shermansdale, and Tim thought how lucky he was to be going to Florida while everybody else went to school.

Uncle Dog had something to say on the subject. "When your Dad and I were young, you couldn't have gotten off school like this. There used to be truant officers who came for school kids that didn't show up. They could even arrest parents for letting it happen."

"Maybe Dad'll get arrested while I'm gone."

"Huh, not these days." Old Dog snickered, "I'd pay a dollar or two to hear that your Mom got locked up for it. Whew, I'd never dare come home again."

Timmy tried to imagine his mother in jail because he had missed school. If that ever happened, he guessed he had better not come home again either.

Arlis Carlisle lay quietly, hoping her husband believed her asleep. Larry was not; she knew his sleep sounds too well to doubt. He, too, was probably thinking about their son, somewhere in the Carolinas by now, off to his first great adventure. Perhaps not though. Larry also had his brother to worry about. Old Dog was seriously ill, so sick he would not survive. Somehow, she had difficulty believing that. Old Dog always survived.

Old Dog was such a trial, but he was like chronic pain. After a while one hardly noticed the misery. Unfortunately, Old Dog simply devastated the Carlisle's social standing. Although no one outwardly criticized or laughed about the family's black sheep, Arlis just knew they snickered behind her back. If someone else had a good-for-nothing biker in their family, Arlis would certainly have noticed, so others did as well.

She could understand male acceptance of Old Dog, although it still surprised her how important men appeared to enjoy Adam's company. Men, after all, were little more than large boys, who still liked to believe themselves brave and adventurous. Dog's loose biker ways titillated them, probably made them feel young and vigorous. Arlis heard herself sniff in practiced contempt.

Once, just once, Old Dog had had a genuine opportunity to make up for his years of sullying the Carlisle name, but every time Arlis thought about it, she almost cried before grinding her teeth in helpless fury.

Old Dog mentioned dozens of rider acquaintances around the country. Most of them had horrid nicknames like Snake, Barf, or Zip. Not all, though, and he occasionally mentioned Malcolm, who lived in New York or maybe Connecticut. Arlis never listened closely.

Just before the annual Harley-Davidson convention in Sturgis, South Dakota—Arlis supposed it was 1989—Old Dog let her know that a number of biking pals, including Malcolm might stop by. He rarely asked, but this time he wondered if she might fix up a nice home-cooked meal for them.

Of course she said, "No!" Arlis Carlisle had let him know that she was not a servant for a bunch of motorcycle bums. Old Dog had shrugged, raised a peace sign, and gone away.

Arlis heard the motorcycles as they turned the corner and came past the Mormon Church. She stepped onto the porch and waited.

There were six of them, new looking machines with leathered and helmeted riders. They braked below the porch, and she stepped to the rail, fists on hips, letting her disapproval show.

"Good morning, ma'am. I'm Malcolm, we're looking for Old Dog." The speaker was an old dog himself, certainly in his sixties, clean shaven and tanned, probably balding under the helmet.

Arlis kept her voice cold. "He lives out back in the shack with the porch."

She closed hard. "Stay off the grass going around." The screen door slammed behind her.

The Harleys rumbled into life, and their thunder rounded the house comer. Arlis peered out the sink window, watching Old Dog vault his porch railing to back slap and shoulder punch his visitors. The riders, Arlis saw, were all old men. They wore glasses and had wrinkly necks. They ought to act their age and stop riding motorcycles, she decided.

Larry and Tim were coming from the barn and stopped for introductions. Timmy climbed the porch, obviously intending to stay. Surprisingly, Larry also picked a spot to settle.

An hour later Arlis heard the cycles firing up. Old Dog led them down the drive where they shifted to two abreast. Her husband and son came in the back door.

While they washed for supper, Arlis put the food on. As usual, they ate in the kitchen where things were handy. When seated in place, Arlis asked, "Where is Dog taking them?"

"Over to the Newport Hotel for supper. Malcolm will have his trucks there to take the motorcycles on to Cleveland. The riders will fly out and join up there for some more visiting."

Timmy was more concerned with machinery. "They had handsome scooters, Dad, but I like Uncle Dog's shovel better."

Arlis's interest had been piqued. "How can they afford to fly around like that? How do they get the money?"

Larry Carlisle's fork froze halfway to his mouth, and he looked a trifle stunned.

Tim said, "That Malcolm's got all the money in the world. He even owns castles and palaces and has some fancy kind of eggs worth millions, doesn't he, Dad?"

A cold knot began forming low in Arlis Carlisle's innards.

Her husband laid his fork down and looked at her in wonderment.

"Arlis, I thought you knew. Dog has mentioned him a hundred times."

She wanted to scream, "Who is he?" but contained herself. It was not easy; Larry was obviously upset by her not knowing.

He cleared his throat, as if unwilling to explain.

"Arlis, Old Dog's Malcolm is Malcolm Forbes, the famous publisher. Tim is right, Mister Forbes is very rich and internationally famous. He and his friends, who are also international personalities, call themselves 'The Capitalist Tools.' They are on their way to Sturgis for the Harley-Davidson gathering and stopped to visit with Old Dog."

Arlis said faintly, "Oh, I didn't catch his name."

She wanted to rage, to throw food on the floor, to rush out and burn Dog's shack to the ground.

What a social triumph she could have had. Malcolm Forbes sitting at her table enjoying a few of her special recipes. Just a few discreet telephone calls with innocent mention of the great man's presence and casual invitation to drop by—no one could ever again have doubted the Larry Carlisle's place in things.

She blamed Old Dog for this. He could have explained, but Dog would rather humiliate her, and let her miss the greatest social coup there could be. Arlis remembered her voice demanding, "Stay off the grass . . ." she feared she would throw up.

Arlis hid her upset and pretended to listen as Larry ranted on and on about how Mister Forbes had said this, how the chairman of the paper company had said that, and what the White House advisor claimed about something else. Eventually the meal ended. She shooed her men away and cleaned up herself.

It was dark when Old Dog motored in alone. Larry joined him, the men laughed, and Dog's boots thumped in and out of his house. Arlis felt horribly left out and neglected.

The Harley chugged into low idle. In a minute Old Dog coasted around the comer. He waved at her silhouette on the porch and called, "See you in a few weeks." She watched his headlight turn left and heard the bike pass through town.

Larry came through the house and sat beside her. After a bit he said, "Dog's off to Sturgis. Going to meet up with Malcolm along the way, if it works out."

Arlis wished silently that Old Dog would never come back.

Timmy came around the house making motorcycle noises and parked on the bottom step.

Larry said, "Just like that, Dog packs a shirt and some socks and starts for South Dakota. Isn't that something?"

Timmy explained, "That's the way real bikers are, Dad. 'They live to ride, and ride to live.'" The boy parroted a Harley-Davidson slogan.

Arlis made the best of it, but just describing to social people how Malcolm Forbes and some industrialists had come by did not really stick. She also prayed for forgiveness of her anger at Old Dog, and a more tentative offering that suggested that she might have been more charitable to her brother-in-law's friends.

Neither gossip nor prayer did much good. Arlis still got heartburn thinking about it.

Larry Carlisle was awake. He could feel the tension in Arlis's still form and supposed she was worried about Timmy being off with Adam and of course the motorcycles she feared with illogical intensity.

The damned things were dangerous but not suicidal. Men rode their whole lifetimes without injury. It was usually a young guy still learning who piled up and made interesting newspaper reading. Not always, though. George Coldren had gotten spilled because his kickstand was down, and George knew how to ride. Larry guessed the point of letting Timmy travel with Old Dog was that he wanted his son to experience things and not live and die in some safely cocooned ignorance. Arlis had not put her foot down, and Larry appreciated that. Old Dog was not her favorite relative, and it took a lot of restraint to see her only son ride off with him.

That Old Dog was hurting did not help. Dog might misjudge and get really ill—it could happen. Larry had made sure Timmy had the office phone number as well as the home phone. When he was working, Larry might not pick up the house phone, and—well, it just paid to be prepared.

Old Dog had reservations at a posh hotel right on the beach, and he had chosen to drive the pickup south. Both were firsts. Dog had usually camped in some place called the Nova Campground, and he always rode his Harley the whole way. Dog obviously wasn't himself.

Tim was in for some wild scenes, that was for certain. Larry hoped the better things Adam would point out and talk about would balance the bizarre, vulgar, and reckless Timmy would encounter.

Larry remembered the easy, worldly competence of a youth whose U. S. Marine Corps father had turned over to his sergeants for maturing. That boy handled everything with exemplary aplomb. Larry Carlisle did not want his son emulating Old Dog's lifestyle—and experience usually helped honest perspective. He hoped and expected that seeing firsthand would remove the mystery, so that Tim could choose and judge with knowledge rather than immature imaginings.

Often when Old Dog took off on a trip, Larry squelched an urge to climb on and leave his own work-day world behind. Riding in the wind, camping under the stars, seeing new faces and places always held attraction. Breakdowns, dirt, public antipathy, mean cops, and foul weather did not. Rootlessness quickly lost its allure for most, and many would-be wanderers developed a hunger for direction and meaning in their lives.

On the other hand, until Old Dog saw the tunnel's end, he had not given a hoot in hell about direction. He might call in from the Florida Keys when they thought he was in Oregon or casually mention just riding in from Saskatoon.

Larry wondered if Adam was often lonely. He found himself grinning in the dark. Perhaps in some higher or subconscious sense Old Dog could be lonesome, but Adam had arrived too many times with long haired, hard-bodied women riding behind. Arlis was predictably offended, more so as Dog aged, and the female companions stayed young.

Male riders regularly rumbled up the drive looking for Old Dog. They came astride an astonishing variety of Harleys, with an occasional foreign machine as spice. The riders were often more outlandish than their rides. Some were powerfully intimidating, huge-bodied and tattooed.

Those kinds made Larry Carlisle think of pillaging vandals. Arlis never got over the giant whose helmet boasted viking-like buffalo horns and who had chrome studs over the knuckles of his fingerless gloves. He wore an elbow-length fur cape attached to his leather jacket and damned if his handle had not been Ragnar.

Rob Troyer out of Florida had a waist-length ponytail that he usually controlled with rubber bands, and his lady's saucy good looks (Bobby-Joe was it?) had about stolen Timmy's heart. Mike, a local Harley dealer, came by occasionally, and he had a gold Harley-Davidson eagle on a front tooth.

When he thought about it, Larry supposed a lot of riders were ordinary-looking guys, but to save his life, he could not recall a dozen. The wild role-players were remembered, just the way most of them intended.

The surprising shared characteristic among the bikers that visited Old Dog was their inherent gentleness. It was as if they went to lengths to show they were not really the bad guys they appeared to be, and Larry learned to enjoy them without trepidation. Arlis never did. They menaced virtually all of her important mores. She was constrained; they gave a damn for very little. Arlis was timid; they hunted adventure. His wife was chaste, circumspect, and modest. The best that could be said was that most bikers were not.

Larry expected that if you tangled with bikers you would not encounter many Marquis of Queensbury rules, and he knew they stuck together like coat hangers.

Their stories were filled with incidents of helping out other riders, often on the road, but sometimes in brushes with the law or antagonistic people. Larry planned on avoiding biker wrath.

Old Dog's riders complained with regularity about their bad press. Movies never had a decent thing to portray, although a famous profile or two did mount Harley-Davidsons to enhance their macho images. Cleaning out biker bars with one-man martial arts performances had become de rigueur, and the cinematic enactments roused both irritation and levity among the real riders.

To tell the truth, Larry liked Dog's friends, and their presence gave his life emotional uplifts that remained in his memory.

What he saw in Daytona would stay in Timmy's memory as well. The father expected his son would file it, just as he did, and be richer for the experience and knowledge—without expecting to become a one percenter, any more than he really expected to be a fireman or a professional wrestler.

Chapter 9

Old Dog's pickup was outwardly beaten and battered. As far as Timmy knew, it had never been washed. If he had something special to haul, Uncle Dog might "broom-out" the truck bed, but mechanically, the Dodge ticked as if new. "Some things count and need taking care of, but a lot of things don't." Old Dog liked to say that. Obviously, the pickup's exterior was among the latter.

Dog drove swiftly, usually a little above the speed limit. Everyone knew police never bothered cars running just a little fast. Old Dog had something to say on the subject.

"In Pennsylvania, it's important to keep an eye out. If you guess wrong and do get pulled over, the fines are painful. Another point we all hate to admit is that most car speedometers run a couple of miles fast, so we either aren't really over the limit or are so darn close it is hard to measure. Most arrests these days are from radar, and police have to worry a little over whether their equipment is all that accurate. So they also give you a little slack.

"There are weird exceptions, of course. Ross got ticketed on Alligator Alley down in Florida for driving two miles over the limit They got Ross with a radar in a helicopter. They were waiting for him at the west tollbooth. Didn't bother cars passing him the whole way. Some cops like arresting bikers. Really ticked old Ross off.

"If a trooper tails you at seventy-five miles per hour, you're done. Hell, a driver like that ought to get nailed for being so stupid."

"Unmarked cars get a lot, Uncle Dog."

"Yep, to me the risk isn't worth the hour you save in a day's run."

The pickup got rotten mileage, and the tank was small, so they stopped often to gas up and stretch. Timmy loaded up on Quicky-Mart junk food. Old Dog had a milkshake and said it was awful.

"Plastic, Tim. I think these fast-food joints have developed a liquid shake plastic by melting down recycled Styrofoam. You notice they call 'em shakes now? Never milkshakes. No cows involved anymore."

Old Dog reminisced. "My mom, your grandmother, worked in Bowers Restaurant for a while when your Dad and I were real young. That's where Mama's Pizza is now.

"She was always trying to fatten us up so we'd grow big and strong. Nobody'd heard of cholesterol back then, and eggs and cream were thought to be good stuff.

"Mom would make us special shakes. She used Half and Half instead of milk and broke a raw egg or two into the mix. Malt was considered healthy, so we usually got that, too. Good rich Hershey's ice cream and a little flavor—man, what a shake! Big, too, at least two glasses. I'd like one of those right now."

Dog had to take a nap about the time they hit I-95. They pulled into a rest area, and Tim roamed around while Old Dog slept. There wasn't much to see, and Timmy was glad when they got back on the road.

Old Dog wanted to quit early, and Tim could tell he was tired, but the South of the Border signs kept them going.

Dog said, "I want it on the record that I'm stopping here for you, nephew. I don't want it passed around that I couldn't wait to get to South of the Border."

"It sounds great, Uncle Dog. Do they have someone dressed up like Pedro?"

"Hey, I'm not up on South of the Border. It isn't my kind of place. Had a friend . . . who was it . . .? Oh, yeah. Cabinets Jim was his handle. So many Jims around you have to add something to know who you're talking about.

"Cabinets went to South of the Border on his honeymoon. He's still married, so I guess for him it was tolerable."

"Why do they call him Cabinets, Uncle Dog?"

"That Jim had a cabinet shop over in Venice, Florida. Nice looking guy. Resembled Robby Benson, the actor."

"Robby Benson's pretty old now, Uncle Dog. I haven't seen him in a recent movie."

"Benson's old, Huh? He's a young guy to me. Depends on where you are looking from, I guess."

Their room wasn't special, but Old Dog said his milkshake was almost decent. He gave Tim money, took a pair of pills, and went to bed.

Tim came in quiet and kept the light off, but Old Dog was awake.

"Can't you sleep, Uncle Dog?"

"Just laying here resting."

"When I rest, I sleep."

"Yeah, well, I do some of both these days."

"Don't you feel good, Uncle Dog?'

"Can't say I do, but it's under control. Gets too bad, I've got pills that ease things."

"You don't have anything real bad, do you Uncle Dog?" Dog could hear the anxiety in Tim's voice.

"It could be worse, Timmy. I'm on my feet, and we're going to Daytona. I'll give you a real clear description when we get back home."

Before the boy could answer, Old Dog shifted subjects.

"How'd you like South of the Border?"

"It's OK, but I don't think I'll want to stop on the way home."

"My sentiments exactly. Some things you've got to see just so you know you won't want to come back."

They got an early start and made good time down the interstate. Old Dog set the needle on 67 mph, and the miles sped by.

There were motorcycles now. A lot of them on trailers and in the backs of pickups, but riders, too. Sometimes a clot of bikers would appear in the side mirrors. They would sweep by, bundled in leathers because the day was only slightly warm.

Old Dog recognized a few. More glanced in as they passed and threw Dog a raised thumb salute. Old Dog answered, but often wasn't sure who they were.

"A lot of riders know you, Uncle Dog."

"I've been around a long time, Timmy."

"How's the gas? I'm getting hungry again."

"My god, you can't be! You just ate a ton at McDonalds."

"There's a Burger King at this exit, Uncle Dog. They're my favorite."

Dog flicked on the turn indicator. "I hope they make decent shakes."

"That all you're going to eat, Uncle Dog? I'd get sick of them."

"Right now they agree with me."

They made it a pit stop, and there was a Dairy Queen next to the Burger King.

Old Dog came back with an ice cream concoction called a Blizzard. "You want one of these, Tim? I'm going to try it instead of a shake."

He began spooning. "Man, that IS good!" Then, "I just hope it doesn't tear up my guts."

"What kind did you get?"

"This one has Oreo cookies broken up in it. I figure they couldn't hurt."

"You'll get fat, Uncle Dog."

"How I wish it."

A dozen miles north of Daytona, Old Dog dropped off I-95. "Too much traffic from here on, and it'll be backed up getting into town."

Dog pointed over a shoulder. "There's the Holiday campground. We'll come up here visiting later on."

The back way in led through a state park and was a pleasant tree-lined drive. Most of the traffic was motorcycles, and Timmy wished they were on the Harley. Once they got into Daytona, it was virtually all motorcycles.

Tim's voice was excited. "I never dreamed of so many bikes, Uncle Dog. This place is ALL Harleys."

"Wait till you see Main Street and wait until Saturday. This is just a preview."

Old Dog's hotel was, Timmy immediately decided, "something else."

Their beat up old pickup with the sheeted over Harley was rolled under a two story high canopy, and uniformed attendants appeared. One took their names and flight bags and disappeared inside the hotel. Another jumped behind the wheel. Old Dog said, "I want to be parked up front where I can roll the scooter off without holding up traffic."

The attendant appeared doubtful. Old Dog tucked a five dollar bill into the man's jacket pocket, and the attendant said, "Well . . ." in a dubious tone. Dog delivered a second bill, and the driver lit up like neon. "Of course, sir. I just thought of the perfect spot." The truck was swallowed by the maw of the parking garage.

Dog looked after the truck, then shook his head in discouragement. "Money talks, doesn't it Tim? Let's go in."

Their room was way up, but the elevator was fast and didn't stink of people and stale smoke the way some did.

Their guide with the bags led into a veritable palace, but Tim hot footed through to the balcony. A sea breeze blew his hair awry, and he could see for a million miles to the north.

Below, an almost too wide to believe beach was awash with people, vendors, and two way traffic. Bathers were way out and still only waist deep. Timmy could barely wait to hit the water.

They each had a bedroom and a shared living room with a TV the size of a wall. The carpet felt like it had no bottom, and the bathroom was enormous. It was tiled to the ceiling and had both shower and whirlpool bath. There was a strange fixture that looked like a commode without a seat. Tim couldn't figure its use. He would ask Old Dog later on.

Dog tipped their "bellhop" and looked around.

"Reckon it'll do?"

Tim did not hide his impression. "It looks like a movie, Uncle Dog. Wow, this must cost a mint."

"Sure doesn't come free, but I'm not up to camping right now."

They went together to study the view. Timmy said, "A lot of bikes on the beach."

"Yeah, we'll be down there later on. We've got a lot of time, and we are right in the middle of things.

"You want to go swimming?"

"Yeah."

"OK, get into your suit. Has it got a pocket? Put in a room key and fistful of quarters so you can get something to eat."

Dog did a little warning. "It's late in the day, so the sun won't eat you up, but come back in an hour, agreed?"

"I'll watch the time, Uncle Dog. My Timex is good down to one hundred meters."

Dog said, "Don't test it. I'll get up after a while. You can watch the tube until then. They've probably got every channel in the world."

The boy took about two minutes and was off. Old Dog swallowed pain pills and slid between the cool sheets. He didn't feel all that bad considering—just bushed. He set his mental clock for not more than two hours and hoped that the dope wouldn't throw him off.

It sure was comfortable, with the breeze blowing through. It had cost like hell, but it was a one-time luxury, something for Tim to remember and tell about. It was worth the money. He wouldn't be needing a lot more anyway.

Money was funny stuff, important as hell when you didn't have it. Not even interesting when there was enough.

Old Dog had never worried about money. When he had gone to war he was just out of high school, and even a private's fifty dollars per month had been sufficient. Dollars had been a little short when he had rumbled out of Bloomfield on his first panhead, but only because he was waiting for Rocky Marciano's next fight.

Rocky Marciano, maybe the greatest heavyweight champion of all time. Killed in a light plane crash . . . God, it must have been twenty-five years back . . . Marciano had been Dog Carlisle's road to financial solvency.

There was a draftee in his basic training outfit out of Brockton, Massachusetts. They had become friends, and the soldier claimed he was close to Rocko Marchegiano, the hard-hitting heavyweight fighter.

The soldier said, "I'll tell you straight out, Dog. Rocky is going to make me rich. Every time he fights, I'm betting every nickel I can beg on him." He whispered confidentially, "I've already got fifteen thousand dollars stashed from it."

Dog was intrigued, but he wasn't much of a betting man. His friend was insistent.

"Look, Dog, you get together all you can and bet with me. All on Rocky winning. No rounds or fancy stuff, just winning. If you lose, I'll pay you back, guaranteed. We're friends, and I want to see you get rich too."

Dog had done it and won, of course, because Marciano never did lose. His friend had gotten out of the service, kept borrowing to the hilt and betting it all. The friend lived in Palm Springs, California now and knew famous personalities.

The winnings were nice, but Dog could not risk the way his Brockton friend could. He banked some and invested in things he thought might get valuable.

Richard S. Otto had been selling house lots at Morro Bay, California. People were flocking to the state, so Dog bought three adjoining properties right over the water for $1,000. Dog got rid of them in 1985 because the taxes were eating him up. They sold as a unit for just under $350,000. The capital gains tax was awful, but Dog didn't care. The investment had been far beyond his expectations. He could not complain, and he didn't really give a damn about the money anyway.

While Rocky was still pounding out opponents, Dog roamed around Florida. He bought a few cheap, but high above sea level lots in the Keys and some others near Tampa. Dog always bought waterfront. It cost a little more, but he figured people liked boats and fishing, and a view ought to bring more down the road. It did. Some sage coined the popular, "They aren't making any more waterfront." The property took off.

Old Dog sold when it seemed right. Probably too soon it turned out, but the money was still nice. Dog tried the stock market in small amounts, but he was just guessing. He settled on ATT for security and IBM for big profit hopes. The gods smiled, and Old Dog lived off his interest.

All because of Rocky Marciano and his 49 consecutive wins. Astonishing how it had turned out. Old Dog claimed no special credit. He had taken chances and been lucky. One solid right cross from any of a dozen opponents might have dumped the Rock and changed it all.

Chapter 10

When Old Dog got up, Timmy had a local station on the TV. In his background the announcer had a motorcycle wreck with emergency vehicles, lights flashing, and police directing. The anchor intoned caution and sobriety.

Tim said, "Somebody got hit hard, Uncle Dog. Looks like he ran smack into the side of a car."

Old Dog swore. "Those bastards, they've been showing that clip for three years now. A Pontiac backed out right in front of the rider. Biker never had a chance. Killed him dead. Car driver was legally drunk and had no insurance. The pictures are damned graphic, so they haul them out every year, but they don't mention that the car was at fault. Hell, they never do."

Old Dog turned away. "Ready to look at bikes?"

"You bet. I've seen a thousand already. The beach is full of them. From all over, too, Uncle Dog. I saw an Oregon plate."

"You'll probably see Alaska. Riders come in from everywhere."

Old Dog slid into his worn leather jacket. It hung on his leaned frame like an old sack.

Timmy said, "You keep losing weight, you'll have to buy a new jacket, Uncle Dog."

"Guess I'll stick with this one a while. We've come a long way together."

Timmy did not have real leathers, but he donned his vinyl jacket with the Harley eagle that Old Dog favored.

"We going to get out the Harley, Uncle Dog?"

"Not tonight. We'll unload in the morning. Tonight's for looking, not riding."

Atlantic Avenue paralleled the beach and Main Street crossed Atlantic. Their hotel lay within spitting distance of the action, so Dog and Timmy skipped through backed up motorcycle traffic to the west side of Atlantic and walked south to Main Street

On the beach side, Main ended abruptly at a pier that cost money to get out on. Heading west, Main Street traffic jerked, started, and halted. The clog of motorcycles was mind boggling.

The traffic was ALL motorcycles—with a few uncomfortable and leery-eyed tourists trapped within the press. An occasional pickup, usually loaded with girls, made the scene and Daytona police were there on foot and astride their own Harley-Davidsons.

Sidewalks were jammed with jacketed lookers. Old Dog said, "If we get separated and can't find each other, I'll meet you on this corner as soon as I can get here, OK?"

"Right, Uncle Dog." Tim's eyes were darting sight to sight.

Police allowed only southbound, right turn traffic onto Main Street. Northbound riders had to pass Main, then "U" turn a few blocks up and blend into the barely-moving south lanes.

Riders trying for Main Street rode feet down, working throttle, clutch, and front brake, staying in low gear, starting and stopping every few feet. The thunder of revving engines was deafening, but to those involved, the ear-shattering decibels were sweet music.

On Main Street, the traffic was as slow as it could get without permanent halting. Few cared; they had come to see and be seen. The usual drill was to ride Main Street a time or two, then park and walk the same few blocks looking at motorcycles, other riders, and lots of scantily-clad motorcycle girls.

The motorcycles were the main attraction: backed into place, shoulder to shoulder, their chromed front ends challenged each other across the busy street. The Harleys posed like chained mastiffs, just waiting their masters' signal.

Harley-Davidson ruled. There were some magnificently equipped Honda Gold Wings, BMWs, Triumphs, and lesser lights, but few eyes paused. The Harley look dominated. Try as they might, no motorcycle company had ever approached Harley-Davidson's appeal.

The attraction was a little difficult to explain. Other machines could claim equal or better mechanics, and every conceivable shape had been tried and was probably present at Daytona.

Many of the Harleys were old bikes like Dog's. Mechanically and technically they were dinosaurs. The old knuckle, flat, pan, and shovel head engines leaked oil, fouled plugs, and required constant tinkering and puttering.

Yet, they had the look. They felt like real motorcycles, and most of all they had the sound A Honda whispered with car-like quiet. Triumphs could be made to spit and pop, but a Harley ... the big twin "V" engines, ancient as the design might be, sounded their beast-like thunder at some primal level and tempo that grabbed a rider's guts and never let go. Everyone, no matter what they rode, understood the hunger for a Harley-Davidson.

The Harley camaraderie was, of course, unique. Honda, Suzuki, Kawasaki and other Rising Sun companies had their clubs and aficionados, but Harley drew from countless wells. Yuppies wore Harley-Davidson clothing and rode Sportsters; a few straddled big twins. People who never rode had Harley T-shirts and Harley-Davidson decals in their rear windows. Harley riders formed brotherhoods that spread tentacles nationwide, and the hottest selling exports to Europe were customized Harley-Davidsons.

Customizing was special to Harley-Davidson motorcycles. Other makes sold a little chrome and a few do-dads. After market Harley parts and equipment were flourishing industries. Shops across the nation specialized in engine modifications, chromed pieces, and exotic paint jobs. A few places did it all.

At least five magazines—*Easyriders*, *In The Wind*, *Harley Women*, *American Iron*, and *The Enthusiast*—pumped Harley riding. The big annual powwow at Daytona epitomized Harley-Davidson. Exciting, adventurous, sometimes outrageous, Bike Week drew the brothers. How much you made or how famous your name was likely to compare poorly with what you rode and where you rode it.

The kings of the Harley fraternity were the old guard, long on the road riders like Old Dog Carlisle. If it had been done, they had been there. Once there had been an older generation that had ridden the earliest of motorcycles, but they were about gone now. The old regulars were now in their fifties, and few, like Old Dog, more than that. Not all old bikers were widely known—many stayed home and rode locally.

The roamers saw a lot of byways and attended many rallies, races, and campings. They were the Harley-Davidson elite, although few of them gave a hoot in hell about the bestowed fame. Doing was important. Their machines held interest, and memories were their crown jewels. What was next hung in the wind for all of them: Rolling Thunder in Washington DC ... 40,000 riders would show up; Americade in New York—a lot would share with the Mom and Pop Gold Wings; then the hoopla of Sturgis in August—everyone wanted to make Sturgis.

Tim began to believe every biker in the world knew his Uncle Dog. Hairy, tattooed, leathered men wrapped arms around Old Dog in bear hug greeting or exuberantly high fived or perhaps just gripped hands in lengthy memory sharing.

Their progress along Main Street was less than a crawl. A lady with many fringes on her jacket and chaps scrubbed Timmy's hair into a snarl, exclaiming, "Hey, Little Dog. Haven't seen you since Jake and I stopped by your place."

Tim could not remember her, but she said he had grown a lot. If they hadn't seen a kid in six months or so, everybody said that. Everybody also scrubbed kids' heads. It was the thing to do, he guessed.

Timmy did like being called Little Dog. Not many called him that, and his mother hated it.

He wondered how he could get the nickname permanent-like. Uncle Dog didn't seem to mind. Sometimes they were called "Old Dog and Young Dog. Tim liked Little Dog best.

After a while, Old Dog suggested that Tim go look at bikes. He would be talking along the street. If Tim couldn't find him, they'd meet where planned in an hour. Tim liked that better. There were things to see and hear.

Leather shops were booming. They opened for the week—then went home. Pins and T-shirts were sold everywhere. Drinking places had hard looking guys in the doorways beside signs that announced, "No Colors and No Attitudes." Colors meant club insignia, of course. There were clubs and even gangs that waged constant battle. During Bike Week, Daytona Beach was declared neutral ground by mutual consent as well as police enforcement, and trouble was rare. There was less violence and fewer accidents than occurred during Spring Break, or Speed

Week when cars raced. The bikers were louder, but rarely obstreperous.

Timmy saw motorcycles that boggled his mind. One big Harley was one hundred percent chrome plated. The ultimate chrome job, the machine was greatly admired, but he also heard, "I wonder if anyone ever sat on the seat." A voice suggested the engine never got turned over, and another added, "If that bike got caught in the rain, the owner would die." Different strokes for different folks applied to Harley-Davidsons.

Old Dog had little use for Harley Sportsters. Dog said that most Sportster riders wished they had a big twin, or they rode sportsters because they were afraid of a real road machine.

Tim liked them just the same. A little smaller in most ways, Sportsters could be purchased with the biggest of engines. Although rough on the butt for lengthy trips, Sportsters handled quicker than their big brothers. For smaller riders, Sportsters made sense. Tim guessed he would start with one.

Old Dog found a seat on Black John's panhead and decided to stay there. His legs felt a little puny and sitting was better.

During a break in conversation he asked, "Anybody remember a rider called Hunch that was around back in the early eighties?"

One guy did. "I try to forget him, Dog. Hunch was dirty. I figure he killed a kid for his ride."

The listeners were attentive, Old Dog among them.

"You remember that ghost town we hung out in one summer, the one up above Silver City?"

"Yeah, it's a tourist trap now."

"You mean like Daytona Beach?" They shared laughter.

"A young guy named Bidwell showed up with a hell of a bike. If a piece could be chromed, it had been. It made everybody drool.

"The kid was quitting, going home to Lincoln, Nebraska.

"Hunch wasn't popular, and the brothers were hinting he should move on. Hunch left with the kid. Next time I saw Hunch was in L. A. He was riding the kid's Harley. Claimed he bought it with his old bike in trade.

"Well, could be. The kid was quitting the road, but Bidwell loved his machine. Anyway, a year later I was in Lincoln, so for the hell of it I looked up the Bidwell family."

The rider paused adding tension to his story. "The kid had never come home."

A listener said, "Holy hell! "

Another said, "Still, he could have . . ."

The storyteller interrupted. "That isn't the end of it. A month or two later, I was eating in a beanery along I-90 and what pulls up is Hunch's old shovel.

"I made talk, and the rider told me how he'd bought the shovel from Hunch because Hunch had a new machine. The guy described the kid's Harley clear to the axles. Fellow's name was Bates out of Denver. I made it a point to remember.

The silence was a little shocked.

"You report it?"

"Naw. I don't know Hunch's name, and it was a cold trail. Family might have listened, but I just let it go."

"Why're you asking about a foul ball like that, Dog?"

"Just wondering where he'd gone to."

A rider laughed, "Stool will know."

"Yeah, anybody seen Stool?"

"He's around. Saw him in the *Easyriders* store last evening."

Old Dog figured Stool might have some Hunch news. Stool absorbed biker information like a computer and never seemed to forget anything.

Dog had a reason for asking, although it had nothing to do with his own encounter long years back with the rider called Hunch.

Chapter 11

They had been easy riding up in Oregon, just seeing country and checking things out. Running back south on Route 101 they had cut off at Garberville and headed west to the ocean. They set up camp on the black sand edging Bear Harbor. Out of nowhere, Hunch came tooling in on a tired-looking shovelhead.

Hunch's tanks had marijuana leaves painted crudely on each side, which few riders thought was either sensitive or wise. Hunch was loud and braggy, and his welcome turned cold before his engine. Most brothers blended in, but Hunch was about as comfortable to be around as barbed wire.

Old Dog had been decades on the road, and his experience in judging strangers had passed from a tentative maybe to almost a sure thing. Dog suffered immediate distrust of the new arrival. He kept his greeting reserved and made no attempt to draw Hunch closer.

Hunch claimed to be from New England, but his accent was South Texas. A lot of brothers fudged on who they were or where they were from, so no one cared.

The stranger had money and flashed it obnoxiously. His talk was crude, and his attempts at jokes were forced efforts that invariably fizzled.

The man was also an interrupter. In the middle of another's yarn, Hunch would butt in with barely relevant trivia that was intended to demonstrate his familiarity with the topic. The guys endured because allowing a man to be himself was part of the informal creed. Bikers came in all persuasions, and to get along they learned to grant more than a little slack.

Then Hunch began getting on Little Pat. That was easy because Pat was small and timid. In pick-up ball, Pat would have been the last chosen. He rode his Sportster poorly and was always out on the fringe of things, sort of just hanging on. But, Little Pat was gentle and decent. From just being around he had become one of the bunch, sort of an unofficial mascot.

When Hunch started bugging Little Pat he looked around for group approval. He got none but kept on anyway. Hunch had been in camp only half an evening, and he was already close to eviction.

Hunch settled in for serious badgering. Pat's Sportster was a baby's machine; Pat's glasses came from Coke bottles; Hunch thought Little Pat's father might have been Italian because Pat's arms looked like spaghetti sticks.

Old Dog suffered Hunch's braying laughter through more than a few bullying commentaries. Brothers shifted uneasily, and Little Pat's pained embarrassment grew difficult to endure.

As the old guy on the ride, Dog had been up front, sort of leading, but there was no appointed chief. Still, eyes began slanting in his direction, and Old Dog guessed he was the one who ought to speak up.

When he had had enough, Dog kept a leash on his feelings, but he made his words bite. He had learned long before, maybe as far back as the Korean War, that it was best to have things clear and straightforward, misunderstandings were fewer, and trouble could sometimes be averted.

He said, "Back off, Hunch. Little Pat's a friend of long standing. We like him the way he is. If you don't, just hit the road."

It would have helped if a few others had voiced their own displeasure, but Old Dog was not surprised when they didn't. It was human nature to let someone else bear the burden. If things got physical, brothers would be all over Hunch, but for the moment they only watched.

For an instant, Hunch appeared stunned. Then his big jawed face began reddening, and he swelled his shoulders making himself appear more formidable.

Hunch was big enough to be intimidating. Probably still in his twenties, a fortyish gut hung over his belt, but he had weight and youth on his side. Big handed and as tall as most, Hunch did not see a lot of trouble in one gray haired oldster sitting sideways on a shovelhead's saddle.

"Who in hell are you to tell me what to do?" Hunch balled his fists.

Dog said, "I'm speaking for everybody. Shut up or ride out." Nods supported Old Dog's right, but Hunch was concentrating on the speaker.

"I don't take s--- from nobody, old man. I ride where I want and say what I want."

Old Dog appeared unperturbed. "That's nice to hear. Real powerful words."

Someone snickered. Hunch heard it, and his eyes meaned down. He made his voice menacing. "You're crowding the wrong guy, old man." He made "old man" sound like an insult.

Old Dog got down to business. His left hand pointed to the only road in or out. "You've used up all the good will we've got, Hunch. Ride out now, or we will dump you and your shovel into the harbor. Then we'll ride out and leave you." Others added, "That's right" and "get going."

Hunch got going . . . straight at his tormentor. His big fists were chest high for punching, and his thick featured head led his charge.

In California, nobody wore helmets, but long riders, who crossed many states and encountered many laws, carried them, usually strapped behind their saddles. Old Dog's black bullet helmet was already unfastened and close to his right hand. When Hunch started, Dog came off the seat, the hard plastic shell in his grip. He swung it close in and fast. Hunch was too late seeing it coming.

Old Dog's aim was right. The helmet's impact along Hunch's skull sounded like the thing had been dropped on concrete. Its solid thunk made men wince. Little Pat almost cried out.

Hunch's ferocious attack ended abruptly. No momentum carried him forward. He appeared to have stepped into an invisible wall.

Fists still raised, Hunch sunk onto his knees. His eyes were a little unfocused, but he did not collapse.

Old Dog took a close look, said, "Oh hell," and brought the helmet around in a wicked back hand against Hunch's forehead. Hunch's head rocked back on his neck, but he again did not fall. Old Dog gave him another, about where the first one had landed.

This time Hunch went. He started forward, but Old Dog's foot shoved him sideward, so he would not bury his face in the sand. Hunch's thick legs slid a little, allowing the unconscious body to flop onto a shoulder.

Old Dog rehung his helmet on the saddle back and straddled his cycle. A brother came close to have a look. "Out cold." That seemed a bit obvious, and a few riders said so.

Dog fired up and pulled his Harley a few yards away. It left Hunch's carcass lying alone.

Someone suggested, "Throw a bucket of water on him."

A voice laughed, "Now who in hell carries a bucket along?"

Old Dog said, "Let him be for a minute." He again got his helmet and walked the few steps to the beach. He waited for the right wave and filled the helmet with sea water. He came back and sat the helmet down and waited.

"Maybe he's dead."

"If he is, we'll take him in and claim he fell off his scooter."

"Yeah, everybody will be happy to believe that. Half the people wish we'd all wreck."

"He isn't dead. Hell, can't you see him breathing?"

"You have to look awful close."

A rider said, "I like Hunch a lot better when he's unconscious."

"Why don't you douse him now, Old Dog?"

"You've seen too many movies. It works a lot better if you don't hurry waking up. I'll dump on him once he starts moving."

"Where'd he come from, anyway?"

"His Harley was parked by a building in Whitethorn. Didn't you see it, for god's sake?"

"I was looking at the girls on the porch."

"The ones who were admiring me?"

"No, those were the grandmas. I mean the daughters." Hunch's still form was receiving little respect.

Hunch's leg twitched, then an arm moved. A brother said, "Watch him, Old Dog, he might have a piece."

Dog said, "You're right." He went over and gave Hunch's pockets a few squeezes.

Another rider poked in Hunch's saddlebags. "Nothin' in here, unless it's real small, Dog."

Hunch began sitting up. Old Dog poured the water over his head, and the man shook himself like a soaked hound.

When he began looking around, Old Dog said, "Take your time. When you are ready, ride out." Hunch did not respond.

Dog took a friend aside. "How about you riding into Whitethorn right now. If this jazbo gets a rifle or looks like he's considering getting even, we ought to know."

"Right." The rider headed for his putt.

A brother had hauled an AR-7 survival rifle from his saddlebag. He looked questioningly at Old Dog.

Dog nodded, "Good idea."

A semi-automatic. 22 caliber, the AR-7 stored itself within its own plastic stock. Its owner slapped the pieces together and waited as Hunch struggled to his feet. Hunch shook his head again as though to clear cobwebs and started to speak.

The rifle owner snapped a half dozen rapid fire rounds into the bay, their stinging reports freezing Hunch's unspoken words.

Riders closed in around Hunch, although Old Dog did not bother.

One gave the still groggy biker an ungentle shove toward his Harley.

"Don't talk, just ride out."

Another added, "And keep going, Hunch. We don't want to hear you coming back."

Hunch's glare was for Old Dog, but he got astride and rode out without defiant words. After a while his motor sound faded in distance.

The peace of their camp had been shattered, and it wasn't the same. Night was close, however, so they would stay.

One suggested, "Let's ease back north to Shelter Cove tomorrow."

The plan met with approval.

Little Pat was even quieter than usual. Old Dog went over and sprawled on an elbow beside him.

"Don't let it get you, Pat. That Hunch is a no good bastard."

The gentle man was still mortified. "I'd give anything to be able to stand up to people like that, Old Dog, but I can't. I never can. I get weak I'm so scared, and I can't make myself do anything."

Dog thought it over for a minute. "Nothing you could do, Pat. If you were a get-even guy you could stick a blade in Hunch while he was asleep." Little Pat shuddered. "Seeing you're not, I figure you'd best try to let it roll off you like water off a duck's back. Hard to do, of course."

Old Dog gave the small figure an easy shoulder slap and rose adding, "We like having you along, Little Pat. We don't want punks like Hunch. You keep that in mind."

Pat said, "Thanks for jumping in, Dog. You know I appreciate it."

Dog waved a hand in acknowledgement. "I expect Hunch'll keep going. Our roads'll cross no doubt, but I figure he'll be a lot more careful in his talk."

Old Dog was half right. Hunch kept going, but their paths did not cross again.

Not, that is, until Old Dog's vigil from the deep timber behind racketeer Bat Stailey's mansion.

Stailey's thugs had whipped the hell out of Old Dog. It had needed a while to get over.

To his family and the rest of the world, Old Dog had taken the licking in stride. They should have known better. Ever since he had healed up, Old Dog had been homing in on Bat Stailey, the figure behind the beating.

It had not been easy. Finding where Stailey lived took time because Stailey was not listed anywhere, and Old Dog did not wish to leave a question trail. He eventually found the gangster's retreat, actually owned by a cohort, on the mountain behind Linglestown. To locate the place, Old Dog had followed Stailey home from a publicized charity occasion.

A lot of drive-bys, over time, in different vehicles, gave Old Dog the layout. The house was walled in front, but had a swimming pool behind. Dog rode the mountain on a little Yamaha trail bike, finding the best ways in and out. He learned to park the cycle and walk down close to a little wooded knoll from which he could see the mansion's back side. Later on he found a handier spot to park his pickup and walk over to the lookout.

Because he planned long but was unsure of what he could or would do, Old Dog left no traces. He neither ate nor drank while spying on the Stailey place. No litter betrayed his position.

He saw Bat Stailey, and a time or two watched him swim in the heated pool. Stailey was never alone, and the house was rarely empty. Old Dog saw the men who had pounded him. The head knocker was Stailey's main man, so Dog found out about him. The thug's last name was Clout. Entertaining. The name truly fit.

One evening Clout came regularly to a back door and appeared to be listening. It was worrisome, and Dog considered fading away, but Clout's expectant manner was also intriguing, so Dog stayed.

Then Hunch stepped from the woods edge, circled the pool, and was admitted to the house. He carried a package. Within minutes he left. Astounded, Old Dog stayed in place. After a few moments he heard a motorcycle crank up higher on the mountain. That was all.

Old Dog had recognized Hunch almost at first glimpse. Hunch had not changed, a little more paunchy and heavier jawed perhaps.

Clearly Hunch was a runner for Bat Stailey. A runner of what and how often? It would be hard to find out both answers.

Hunch came once a month, always in the last week. His packages appeared identical. Dope? Stailey would not be that stupid. Money? Maybe. What else was there?

Old Dog found Hunch's motorcycle while its rider was delivering. Hunch rode a quieted down Kawasaki off-road machine. The muffler was huge and very effective. Hunch did not announce his coming.

Backtracking the man proved impractical. Hunch rode different trails and cut cross country. Dog could not effectively follow. He tried guessing and waiting at likely come out spots. No Hunch. Dog decided to let that part go. It was Stailey that he was after.

Hunch had one careless habit. He always hurtled down a last hundred yard swath through the trees and parked in the same place. Old Dog went through his saddlebags. Bingo!

On most occasions Hunch carried a saddlebag packed tightly with a plastic pack of marijuana. Dog guessed Hunch had his own agenda, as well as delivering for Bat Stailey.

Maybe Hunch did bring in Mary Jane for Stailey's personal crowd, but Old Dog found it hard to believe. Stailey was under both state and federal magnifying glasses. He had already been tried twice under RICO laws and been acquitted both times. Stailey was one of the courthouse steps proclaimers who appeared to be above the law. Maybe, Old Dog thought, that could change.

After almost a decade, the nearly forgotten Hunch had reappeared right in Old Dog's sights.

Dog hoped his biker brothers might have information about him that could be useful.

The story of Hunch's murder of the young biker was both hateful and interesting. Dog wondered if Stool, the walking computer, might add something more.

Chapter 12

Old Dog and his nephew closed out the evening with a short walk along Daytona's beach. Traffic was gone, but couples still communed with sand, sea, and each other. Diners and a few fishermen kept the pier busy, and the boardwalk and cement walk teemed with leather jacketed bikers seeking action.

A giant bungee jump drew a crowd of spectators, and a respectable line of jumpers waited turns to hurl their bodies into space to be snatched from destruction—seemingly at the last instant—by the springy bungee cord attached to their ankles. It was a heady ride, and watchers oohed and cheered the daredevil jumpers.

Tim said, "Wow, Uncle Dog, would I like to do that!"

Dog suggested they sit a while and watch. Even the gentlest strolling left him a touch weary.

Dog visualized cancer cells that looked a lot like "Pac men", chewing at his muscle and fiber.

His voice wistful, Timmy said, "I guess it costs a lot to jump."

"Big money, sixty-five dollars for a few seconds thrill."

A failed jumper came back down in the car that had taken him up. Except for a few groans, the crowd spared the embarrassed youth additional mortification.

Old Dog said, "Now that would be a bad memory for life. That guy will never forget the time he wimped out at Daytona." Dog shrugged, "Well, maybe it'll make him gutsier the next time he's faced with a scary situation. He'll recall how lousy it is to fail because he was afraid to try."

Timmy said, "I wouldn't be scared."

"I suspect you would be, Tim. It isn't natural to step off a high place. The question is, could you dive off anyway?"

Detecting a serious note in his uncle's voice, the boy answered with some care. "I guess I would be scared, but with everyone looking I'd go off anyway. I know I would."

"Uh huh. That's what the guy that rode back down thought."

"You ever bungee jump, Uncle Dog?"

"Sure. Right here about three years ago when it was brand new. I went twice, it was so exciting. I didn't have more money on me, or I'd have gone again. It's cheaper after the first jump, but not that cheap.

"I could do it. I'll bet no other kid in my school has bungee jumped."

"Probably not, but it sure wouldn't do to get up there and lose heart"

"I'd do it."

They watched as a jumper swan dived and fell like a stone before the stretchy cord snatched him more than half way back up. Timmy said, "Wow!"

Old Dog nodded, as if making a decision.

"OK, Tim. I'll pay if you really want to jump. Only thing is, I want to be sure you'll do it. Riding back down isn't Carlisle style."

Timmy was on his feet.

Dog said, "Hold it a minute. We've got to talk a little." Tim perched on the bench edge.

Old Dog looked up at the jump. "When you go up, if you decide to go, the man in the car with you will say 'Don't look down.' Well, that's one way, I guess, but the right way to do a thing is to look it straight in the eye. Know what it is you are facing. Know just what you are going to do, then do it.

"So, my advice is, look down, look out, and see that you are above the tallest buildings. Feel the car sway and suck in the cool air up there. You'll feel everybody watching and rooting for you. Realize that you are in the middle of a great adventure and enjoy how scared you are. Then, dive off. Timmy, it's a thriller."

The boy was writhing in anticipation, so they went over and got in line. While they waited, Old Dog added, "Now remember a last thing, Timmy. Nobody EVER gets hurt doing this here at Daytona. One accident and this ride is off the beach and out of business. The danger is all in your head. It isn't real, it just seems real."

When they got close, Old Dog said, "If they ask, tell 'em I'm your Dad so they don't get nervous about somebody as young as you going."

A sharp-eyed, no-nonsense woman sat them down and shoved pre-prepared forms at Old Dog. She said "ID" and Old Dog dug out his driver's license. Timmy showed what he had, and the woman spared them a toothy smile.

"Sign here, initial here, sign here, and here, and here." Old Dog kept signing. He said to Timmy, "I think I just gave away the farm." The clerk had heard it before.

She said, "If you don't jump, we bring you straight down, and it is just as if you did jump, that clear? No money back." Tim and Old Dog answered, "Yes, Ma'am."

Dog paid, and Timmy sat on a tin chair waiting to be rigged out.

The operation was professional and ran like a well-tuned clock. Time was money, and the system was expensive.

A giant crane—over two hundred feet high, they advertised—hauled an open elevator car very high. The jumper stepped out onto a foot-square platform and on signal made his dive. It sounded easy, but most people steered clear, afraid to try. Old Dog prayed Tim would succeed because either way, the boy would remember it.

A youthful attendant strapped Velcro leggings tightly to each of Timmy's calves. At the bottom, each legging had a heavy loop sewed in. The bungee cord would hook through them. A belt was strapped to Timmy's waist. A thin wire with a loop in the end of it dangled from the belt. It was easy to figure out. If the ankle leggings let go, the stainless wire would still save him.

The attendant talked a lot. "Boy, are you in for a great ride. I go every chance I get." Timmy listened, even though he knew it was mostly chatter designed to keep jumpers calm.

He had already been weighed, but as he was led to an "on deck" chair, they weighed him again and checked to see that this weight matched a color sticker placed on his jacket. That was also plain enough. The color sticker matched the color of the bungee cord they would use for him. Each cord would have a different stretch. Too stiff a cord would shorten the fall and give a terrible jerk. Too stretchy a cord might put the jumper into the concrete. The realization raised goose bumps.

It was his turn. The "on deck" attendant, mouth working in encouragement, marched him close. His color cord was attached to the car and the other end to his ankles and the thin wire. The new attendant snapped a wire fastened to the car side to his belt. They did not want a panicky jumper trying to get out at the wrong altitude.

The jump attendant started talking, and the car started up. Along with encouragements came the advice not to look down.

Timmy said, "I want to look down."

The attendant was flexible and adjusted easily. He hated stickers. Keep 'em happy and get them airborne was his job.

Tim tried to see Old Dog, but there was a blur of black jackets. Must be a thousand, he thought, and a nifty idea came to him. Tim wondered if he could do it. He would try.

It was high, and it got higher. Tim found himself squeezing the car rail and made himself let go. The bungee cord ran from his ankles out under the elevator's wire door and came up through the floor. The secure end was fastened where the jump attendant could see it.

The car jerked to a stop and swung giddily. The attendant let it settle down. He unhitched Timmy's security wire. It was time to jump.

Timmy could hear his heart. It thundered in his ears. To each side he could see the roofs of hotels running for miles up and down the beach. The solid motorcycle traffic on route A1A hurled sound and light at him. Ahead, the ocean lay calm and the beach appeared to be a mile or so almost straight down.

The attendant said, "OK, you step out onto the platform. I'll give you a '3, 2, 1, Go.' You dive off and holler 'Bungee' as loud as you can. Ready?"

Timmy nodded because his throat had gone desert dry.

He shuffled onto the tiny platform, holding tight to the car rails, fearful that the swaying and the weight of the cord would pull his feet from under him. The attendant said, "3," and Timmy felt his knees weaken. His mind asked, "Why am I doing this?"

"2," and Timmy thought about Uncle Dog watching. "1!" He forced his fingers from their iron grip on the rails.

"Go!" A hundred thoughts flashed. He could not go—he was so alone with all those people staring—he would jump even if it killed him. He felt his arms shoving sideward into the swan position, but he did not yell "Bungee." Instead, he pushed off hard into his dive, doing his best with the idea he had thought of riding up.

200 feet above, Timmy's small body began its fall into hundreds of upturned faces. His boyish voice came shrill but clear, a call dear to the watcher's hearts. "*HARLEY-DAVIDSON!*"

The magical words struck with nuclear impact. The massed black jackets responded with a roar of approval that startled even the jaded—seen too many—attendants.

Old Dog had made himself sit down and wait it out, but Timmy's appearance on the platform knotted his muscles. The boy's dive started him to his feet, and Timmy's totally unexpected and magnificent "Harley-Davidson" opened Dog's own exultant bellow of satisfaction.

Timmy fell like a rock. The scene blurred, and the crowd's massive response was lost in the instinctive panic of the fall.

His mind screamed, "Too long," even as the bungee began slowing his fall. The ride eased, then, almost as exhilarating, he was hauled back up by the bungee's retraction. The lighted frame of the crane sped past his staring eyes, and he was suddenly looking closely at the bottom of the elevator car. Timmy said aloud, "My gosh what a ride!" Then he was again falling away.

Old Dog watched his nephew bounce at the bungee's end in decreasing rides until he hung from his ankles, arms dangling. The elevator car descended rapidly, and the attendants grasped Timmy's hands, guiding him onto a padded platform. The bungee was unhooked, and the car swung away to meet the next jumper.

Timmy passed through dozens of back slaps and "great jumps" until he found Old Dog. Eyes aglow, he said, "Wow!" Then not satisfied, he said again, "Wow, Uncle Dog." He rushed the last yard to squeeze his uncle in an enthusiastic bear hug. Old Dog squeezed back.

While Old Dog sipped a final milkshake, Timmy devoured a New England style hot dog, with the dog sliced in half and the roll genuinely grilled in butter. Timmy had Thrasher's peanut oil cooked French fries on the side and a Doctor Pepper to wash it all down. Old Dog envied him mightily.

Timmy hashed and rehashed the bungee jump, but he ran out of things to say before they reached their room. For Old Dog it was all good to hear. Tim was just the right age. Another year and he would be too teen-age sophisticated to admit to thorough enjoyment. Enthusiasm would begin to embarrass him. A year or so more and he would be "cool," certain that he knew about everything, and probably a royal pain in the butt. Those phases, too, were part of growing up, and about every boy had to pass through them. Dog was certain he liked this Timmy Carlisle the best

Old Dog took pills and a shower. "I'll likely sleep late, Tim. You can hit the beach, and we'll get the scooter unloaded when I get up. You got money left?"

"I didn't spend much, Uncle Dog."

Old Dog was drifting into sleep when Timmy's voice came through the dark.

"I did it, Uncle Dog. I bungeed."

"You surely did, and the yell was the greatest. Super job, Timmy."

Dog was again almost gone when the boy said, but mostly to himself, "And it was a two hundred footer, not one of those little old bungees they have at fairs."

Chapter 13

In the morning they started early. Old Dog drafted hotel staff to help back the Harley down the ramp. Of course money changed hands.

The weather was brisk, and only the most dedicated were up and parked along Main Street. Old Dog tooled west, pausing to speak with a single acquaintance. He asked about Stool, but the biker had not seen him.

Dog said, "We'll ride out to the fairgrounds, Tim. Things will be stirring out there." He pursed lips in thought. "It's too cold for those denims. Time you got leathers, anyway."

Timmy's heart jumped. His own jacket! They had priced motorcycle jackets, and one made in Pakistan could be had for a hundred and fifty dollars. A real Harley Davidson would cost over two hundred and fifty. Timmy could see little difference in the garments, and he would settle for either.

The ride to the county fairgrounds was long. It was fast highway riding, and the wind bit hard. Tim pressed tight against Old Dog's back, and stuffed his hands deep into his uncle's side pockets. It was still cold, and he was glad when they arrived.

It cost Old Dog eight bucks just to get into the swap meet, but Tim knew instantly that the show was worth every dollar. Spread through acres of open selling stands were millions of motorcycle parts. Cycles were for sale, and there were areas broken down by bike types, where individuals could park their "For Sale" machines.

Old Dog

Within the fairground buildings specialty dealers hawked their wares. Leather and pins, of course, but also chrome, cycle lifts, saddles, engraving, and tattoo artists.

Dog said, "First we'll get you a jacket. Should have done it last night."

Like most things he went at, Old Dog bought fast. He strode up to a leather shop and said, "Pick out the one you like, Tim."

The boy knew what he wanted, one just like Dog's. He tried sizes until one fit.

Old Dog examined the choice. "Looks right.

"Want an eagle or something sewed on?"

Yep, just like his Uncle Dog's.

Dog said, "Gerry out of Nokomis picked my eagle. Gerry's old and rides a Honda, but we let him hang around. He's got good taste in eagles."

Dog asked the vendor how much. The man said, "The jacket's $155 and the eagle's $30 sewed on." Tim choked a little and said out loud that $185 was a lot of money.

Old Dog did not hesitate. "That's too much. I'll pay $170. If that's too little for you, we'll just work on down the line until we get it."

The vendor was defensive. "Hell, I won't make a dime."

Unrelenting, "It's up to you. That's all I'll pay." Dog waited.

The leather man said, "Give me five more for doing the sewing and it's a deal."

Dog smiled, "Deal! What's five bucks between friends." The merchant reached for the jacket and eagle, but Dog's hand lay on them.

Still smiling, Dog added, "Providing we get ten bucks off on a pair of chaps."

The seller groaned, but how could he say "No."

Chaps! Timmy's knees trembled. He had never expected chaps. His uncle handed him the right amount of money. "You pick 'em, Tim. See that guy selling tailpipes? I'll be over there."

Tim went chaps looking, and Old Dog hailed a friend.

The tailpipe peddler was called BC. He said, "Dog, you old bastard. I wondered when you'd show up." He let go of Dog for a closer look. "Damn, you looked peaked. You been sick or are you in training?"

"I've been better, BC. You look well fed, as usual."

"I've got a good woman, Dog. Married life agrees with me."

"Looks like it." Old Dog sat on a display table. "Damn, you still riding that ratted out old hog?"

BC's machine was almost famous. It featured lights. A truck battery replaced a saddlebag. It took a lot of electricity to keep the many bulbs glowing. In daylight, the Harley looked like a two-wheeled junkyard, but at night, with the Christmas strings blinking and strobes flashing, BC's creation stood out.

He also had a horn. It was one of those things big RVs sported—that played a dozen or so recognizable tunes like "Hail to the Chief" and "The Old Gray Mare." You knew when BC was around.

"You seen Stool?"

"I could locate him. What's in it for me?"

"Talk or I'll cut some of your wires."

"Hell, Dog, Stool's sitting over there, almost behind you." Dog looked and there was Stool.

Dog kept an eye on Stool, swapping a year's adventures with BC, waiting for Tim's arrival.

The boy came, self-conscious in his new leathers, flushed with excitement and enthusiasm. He stood for inspection.

BC said, "Kid looks like you must've looked at that age, Dog."

"Ought to. Tim's my brother's boy. Carlisle genes run strong."

They left BC and stood aside waiting because Stool was deep in conversation.

Tim unawaredly ran his hands over the zippers and snaps on his leathers. "Why is he called Stool, Uncle Dog?"

"Well," Old Dog found a seat on a wooden crate. "Years back, Stool had one of those seats that horse people and bird watchers carry around. It had a round padded seat and one long pointed rod for a leg. You stuck the rod in the ground and sat comfortable.

"Stool took the damned thing everywhere. While the rest of us got our butts damp, Stool perched comfortable. Unfortunately, we always had to wait while Stool put his seat away or got it out. Everybody grumbled about it.

"One day up at P-town, out on the end of Cape Cod, we were set up on a beach that had deep sand. Stool was away for a minute, and a big guy sat on his seat. The thing sunk into the sand pretty far, so the guy dropped himself on it, and the stool went deeper. It was a good game, and we all joined in. When he got back, Stool found his seat pounded so deep it was flush with the sand. Took him a hell of a time to dig it out."

Tim laughed, imagining the scene. "He must have been mad."

"A little madder the next time it happened. Guarding his stool got to be more trouble than it was worth. Anyway, some brothers drove it deep on a Jersey beach, and Stool just left it. Probably still there."

Stool looked intellectual. He was a small man, baldheaded, and he wore round glasses. Old Dog said, "Stool's never forgotten anything, and he stores everything he hears. Some claim Stool worked for the CIA before becoming a full-time biker. Now riders tip him for information about their friends or perhaps for advice on where to ride or how to find something."

Dog called, "Hey, Stool."

Timmy swore he could feel Stool's brain shifting gears and focusing on Old Dog Carlisle's file.

"Hey, Old Dog," hesitation, "Gee, you look like hell—man, you're down to fighting trim."

Timmy watched Stool's features tighten as the thickly glassed eyes studied his uncle.

Stool's voice was concerned, "You're seeing a doctor aren't you, Dog?"

"Yeah, I'm being worked on." Tim did not see Old Dog's warning gesture, but Stool changed subjects abruptly.

He shook Dog's hand and studied Timmy for a short moment. "Obviously a relative. Could be your brother . . . Larry's boy."

Timmy said, "Wow!" Stool appeared gratified.

Old Dog and Stool swapped a few incidents of common interest before Dog raised his question.

"You got anything on a rider called Hunch? He was around a few years back, out on the west coast was where I saw him."

Stool seemed to blank over; going deep, Timmy guessed. Stool could make a fortune on the TV game shows.

"Hunch, yeah." Stool came to abruptly. "Bad dude, Dog." A file opened. "Hell, you had a run in with him. Kicked his butt and ran him off. Something about . . . ." Stool searched, Old Dog helped out.

"He was abusing Little Pat."

"That's right." Stool swerved. "Pat's gone to ground in Ogden, the town outside Fort Riley, in Kansas. Operates a gas station."

"Good. Little Pat wasn't really tough enough for the road."

"He still rides a Sportster, though."

"What about Hunch?"

"Hunch . . . did time for cutting a man. In La Jolla, six months, I think. Got ninety days for growing marijuana, up north, around Mendicino. Let's see . . . uh huh, Sacramento police were looking for him, had to do with another stabbing. Bad hombre, Old Dog."

"Got anything more recent, Stool?"

"Only other thing I've heard is that Hunch was drug running back east here. In deep, somebody . . . uh huh, it was Elbow Harley mentioned it, maybe a year ago."

A host of riders claimed to be named Harley Davidson. Some could legally prove it. It was convenient to label the many Harleys out there, and Elbow Harley had gotten broken up in a crash. His left arm had been hurt and would not straighten. His motorcycle had mismatched handlebars, the left one shorter so the rider's hand could reach the clutch, light dimmer, horn, and turn indicator. Old Dog had only heard of him.

Dog said, "Here's an update, but forget the source, unless it's important to mention."

Stool's head was bobbing. Information was like a drug to Stool. He wanted it all.

"Hunch is running under the name Joe Watson. I got that off some bills and papers in his saddlebag." Because Stool would value it, Dog threw in, "Hunch is riding a Kawasaki dirt bike rigged for road use.

"Hunch was carrying a few pounds of marijuana when I checked him out, but he was delivering . . . I don't know what . . . to a big-time criminal, Bat Stailey, up in Harrisburg, Pennsylvania."

"Uh huh, up in your country, Dog. Bat Stailey . . ." Stool thought about it.

"Uh huh, a Teflon Don. Nobody can nail him. Been tried, but he gets off. Probably into everything crooked. Tall, regal looking, with million dollar gray hair. That the guy, Dog?"

"That's him."

Old Dog added, "They're riding in the barrel, Timmy. Go see it. It's a show worth watching. I'll be here with Stool when you're done."

Stool watched the boy go. "Fine young sprout, Dog. You told him yet?"

"Told him what, Stool?"

"About what's wrong with you?"

Old Dog studied his friend in amazement

"Stool, you ought to get a glass ball and tell fortunes. What do you think is wrong with me?"

"Hell, Dog, the signs are there. You're going downhill fast. Think I didn't see you hunt a seat because you felt weak legged? You've got a certain look, Dog. Real sick people get it."

Stool shrugged, "I could be wrong, Dog, but I don't think so."

Old Dog sighed, "I hoped it wouldn't show for a while yet."

"It doesn't much. Few will realize. What is it, AIDS or cancer?"

"God, you should take up doctoring. It's cancer. The big C. Way beyond curing."

"Sorry, Dog, real sorry."

"Yeah, but what the hell, Stool. Life's been good. Quality should count as much as quantity."

"Exactly right, Adam, but it's natural to want more."

How in hell did Stool know his real name? The man was uncanny. Mentioned one time within Stool's hearing, probably; filed and never forgotten.

Stool asked, "Considering your condition, why are you interested in Hunch . . . Joe Watson? " Stool reinforced his memory.

Old Dog had never verbalized his thoughts, much less his half formed plan. He took time to organize.

"Hunch just sort of fell into the picture, Stool. I'm focusing on Bat Stailey."

Old Dog seemed to wander, "Ever think that given the chance, a man ought to do at least one special, distinctive thing for the good of humanity?"

Before Stool could answer, Old Dog went on. "Consider an animal like Bat Stailey. Law can't reach him. He owns better lawyers than the government can employ.

Stailey is chauffeured in a bulletproof limousine that belongs to a "friend." He lives in a mansion belonging to another "friend." Stailey never carries money and has no credit cards. He wears friends' suits, and is always a free guest at social functions.

"Stailey has no paper trail. Yet everybody knows that he is a criminal and a gangster. The one time a colleague agreed to testify against him, the witness's mother and father disappeared and didn't show up until the guy forgot his testimony. Stailey plays real hardball.

"Maybe a person like that ought to be taken care of by concerned citizens."

"Vigilantes ride. That it?"

"Sort of."

"Dangerous stuff, Dog. The old west is long dead. Modem vigilantes would tell their wives or brag to a friend, and other well-meaning people would have to declare the vigilantes guilty of doing the bad guy in and see that they got locked up."

Stool remembered. "There was one incident out in the mid-west where a town bully was shot dead in front of half the populace, but no one would admit to seeing anything. Case never has been settled. I think secret keeping is mighty rare though, Dog."

"I'm dying anyway, Stool."

"You mean do it alone? Snipe the guy from long range, maybe?"

"Maybe, but that doesn't seem like enough. He wouldn't know what hit him, and no clear and certain warning would be delivered for other criminals to think about."

"What do you want, Dog, a high noon shootout?"

Stool chuckled a little. "Tall in the saddle stranger rides into town and plugs the dastardly villain before riding into the sunset. Sounds macho, Old Dog, but hard to arrange, and damned hard to get away with. Hell, brother, you don't want to die in a penitentiary."

Dog said, "I damned sure don't. Guess I'll wear a bandanna over my nose."

Stool snickered, "Great disguise. It's worked in a thousand westerns."

"I've got something else new for your Hunch file, Stool." Old Dog repeated the rider's story about Hunch probably killing the young rider for his fine motorcycle.

Dog added, "I think I'll give the Bidwell family a call and see if their boy ever turned up."

Stool was instantly intrigued. "Let's do it now, Dog. I'd like to know if Hunch really murdered for a motorcycle. If that boy never did show up, I'd say a case could be made. Well, not a court case, but enough to let brothers know."

"A case good enough for a vigilante, Stool? I'll round up Timmy, and we'll make the call."

The Bidwells were still in Lincoln. Old Dog talked first to the mother, then to the father. The son had simply disappeared. He had written that he was coming home, but he had never arrived. Could the caller shed any light on their boy's whereabouts?

Old Dog's heart cried for them, but what good would it do to tell what he suspected. Dog said he had no news and was just checking in.

"The boy never showed up, Stool."

"That should clinch it. If the boy's stayed missing all these years, Hunch killed him for his scooter. But, how do you prove it? Hell, Hunch probably doesn't even have the bike anymore. The law won't help."

"Sounds like a job for 'The Lone Stranger' to me." Old Dog struck a gunfighter's pose.

Stool was not impressed. "You'd better think it over, Adam. Taking out a few bad ones won't change a thing, but it could make your last months miserable."

Old Dog paraphrased, "If not now, when? If not I, who?"

When they got back to Stool's chosen spot a few impatient riders waited.

Dog tucked a hundred dollar bill into his friend's shirt pocket.

"Oh man, that's way too much, Dog."

Dog shrugged, "I've got enough, brother, and, you know, Stool, somehow money doesn't seem all that important right now.

Old Dog bought a motorcycle. He chose an ugly, beat up Yamaha that did not even have a title. Despite its trashed appearance, the machine ran powerfully. Dog rode it around, broadsliding and doing wheelies. The seller said, "If I had papers, it'd be worth money."

"Where'd you get it?"

The seller was vague. "A guy I know had it."

"I'll use it for parts. Old Dog paid $200. Timmy asked, "What the heck is that for, Uncle Dog?" He feared

Old Dog was buying the junker for him, and rat bikes were not his style.

Dog was as vague as the seller. "I know a guy who can use it."

Timmy hoped the guy wasn't him. The Yamaha was hot, and Old Dog had ridden it like he must have when he was young, but Tim Carlisle planned on being a Harley man—period!

Chapter 14

Days blended. Bikers came to Old Dog's hotel to groan at the decadent splendor and to shower. They drank Dog's beer and swapped yarns. Stories ran the gamut of astonishing to vulgarly gross. All were interesting to Timmy Carlisle, although many burned his ears, and he was embarrassed that Uncle Dog knew he heard such stuff.

They also rode, up and down the beach, along Atlantic Avenue, and out Main Street. Faces became familiar to Tim, and it was not unusual for a hairy mountain man biker to clap his shoulder and say, "Hey, Little Dog, where's the old guy?" Or perhaps a massive tattooed arm of weather-coarsened hide would encircle him and ask how he was doing. Timmy loved those occasions.

He met a friend, son of a younger rider, and they worked the beach together. Tim's body browned under the daily sun dosages, and his hair began to bleach. He only thought of home when Old Dog reminded him of his obligation to telephone.

On Friday they rode north to the Holiday Campground. The camp was packed with bikers, but there were also trailers permanently set in place—folks who had nothing to do with Bike Week.

Old Dog settled in for visiting with cycle enthusiasts who did not live the biker lifestyle. Larry, Gary, and Scott were full-time mechanics. They owned Harleys and rode a lot, but their lives were settled on goals other than seeing new places and other riders. But, Old Dog knew them; Tim Carlisle's suspicion that his Uncle knew everybody worth knowing was reinforced.

As dusk came down a rowdy pack of youthful celebrants livened the occasion.

Their camp was a disgraceful mélange of patched up tents and construction plastic stretched among trees and broken off branches to form shelters—possibly adequate to resist morning dew. A tragic collection of trashed out Japanese motorcycles surrounded the encampment providing a protective cordon against other passing barbarians.

Their campfire was, however, truly noble. A half cord of cut and split wood had been brought along, and the noisy gathering enjoyed a monumental blaze worthy of a city's pillaging.

Also notable were the beer coolers. Each participant appeared to have vied to provide the largest.

The group's beer-numbed entertainment was to ride a small Honda motorcycle straight into a nearby palmetto thicket—to see who could penetrate the furthest.

Each attempt ended in a crash with punctures and slashes from the sharp-edged palmetto fronds. Inevitably, a rider ricocheted and sprawled in the magnificent campfire. Singed and scraped the rider submitted to his friends' first aid—a thorough smearing with motor oil—and he was ready to try again.

The Honda refused to die, and the game finally ended in the dark with a thrown rider so deep in sharp palmettos he could not get out. His cohorts held the still running Honda over their heads, using the headlight as a searchlight, helping the lost rider find his way.

It was a good show, and only a too close roll of thunder announced to participants and watchers that a Florida downpour was en route.

Old Dog said, "Oh hell, I hate to ride in the rain." He hustled Timmy into his jacket and dug a face mask from a saddlebag. Dog resisted offers to stay in a tent or a camper for the night and started off. They had barely crossed I-95 when the rain began.

Like many Florida storms, the rain came as a gully washer. Old Dog cut back to about 35 mph and endured the drenching. The water quickly soaked leather, padded linings, and clothing beneath. Chaps, jackets, and plastic face mask took away the sting of raindrops at speed, but the going was treacherous with puddles forming and wet leaves plastered blanket-like on the roadway.

By the time they swung onto A1A, Old Dog's scooter had the highway to itself. Anyone who could was under cover. They made good time to the hotel and up the elevator.

Dog said, "Hit that shower fast, pal. I'm half frozen. When you're done, leave it running hot. I'll be waiting."

Warmed and dried, they watched a little TV, but Old Dog said he was done in and hit the sack. Later, Timmy heard him coughing, and that worried the boy. His uncle was sick. Seriously sick, Timmy believed. How serious, he avoided guessing.

Their last excitement was the Sunday motorcycle parade out to the racetrack. Old Dog stayed for it because he wanted Tim to have seen it all.

Dog rode to the head of the parade and hollered, "Make me a place, bros." Riders greeted and complained and shuffled machinery until Old Dog had a hole. Then they visited, waiting the start.

The front of the parade rode swiftly, the air thunderous with Harley engines. Police escorted, and arrival at the speedway was swift. Old Dog pulled out of line early and parked. "We'll watch 'em go by, Tim."

Motorcycles, mostly Harley-Davidsons, rumbled past for more than an hour. The number of bikes was barely believable. Old Dog said, "And you've got to remember that most of the riders are already gone. A lot can't hang around this long."

They rode slowly on nearly deserted roads back through Daytona and onto the beach for one last tour. Without the massed motorcycles and leathered riders the beach was subdued. In town leather shops were already closed. The stores would reopen on the morrow selling different wares.

Old Dog again rode the Harley onto the truck bed. This time the ramp was steep with no bank to start from. Timmy held his breath, but his uncle made it look easy.

Helpers hoisted the Yamaha alongside the Harley, and Dog tied it down.

Then they were off. Rain threatened but did not return. Old Dog nursed a raspy cough with Hall's Mentholated Drops and said he had best get down to see Doc Klein when they got home.

Timmy was as pooped as Old Dog was, and the boy slept through a lot of the first day's travel. Dog had time to think, and he felt a need to do a lot of it.

Daytona had been all that he had hoped. He had seen a lot of friends and heard some things about others. Timmy, he thought, had a memory to treasure.

A few riders had died since last year. They always had. Statistics said that seventy percent of motorcycle deaths were caused by automobiles at fault. Over the years, cars had taken more of his acquaintances than Old Dog cared to remember. Still, the brothers knew the risks. If you rode, you accepted them. Bikers like himself who rode long distances and year round automatically faced the greater odds. No one Dog knew of wished to be injured or dead, but they believed the freedom of easyriding, the adventure, perhaps the dangers themselves were worth the risks. Some paid heavy dues.

Yet, here he was with forty years of putting, and he was likely to die in bed—if he chose to. "No man knoweth the day or the hour" was usually true. In his thoughts, Old Dog emphasized *usually*, because in this age the *when* did not have to be a final mystery. Man had learned how to comfortably turn off life's spigot, if he chose to.

What about Bat Stailey and Hunch—whatever his real name was? That, to Old Dog, remained an important question.

But why should he care? Within a dozen weeks he would be gone.

What a foreign concept. Intellectually he knew it to be true, but his being, something way in deep, fought that certainty.

The world would grind relentlessly onward, unaffected by Adam Carlisle's demise or by anything he might attempt before then. Perhaps he simply wanted to get even. Vengeance was not often seen as a commendable goal. Because a thing felt good did not make it right. Everyone knew that.

Old Dog smirked at his own reasoning. As strong an argument could be made that inaction was only laziness, uncaring, or even cowardice. "A man did what a man had to do." Real John Wayne thinking there. Old Dog suffered through a coughing fit and sucked on another lozenger.

It pleased Old Dog that Timmy ran first to his mother. He did not want Arlis remembering him only as a wedge between her and her son. The two disappeared into their kitchen, Timmy's squeaky voice rattling away in excited and enthusiastic description. The timing of the Daytona trip had turned out about right.

Old Dog's belly hurt with a grim ache, as if a fist deliberately squeezed his guts. He had a little chest pain as well. It was a first and, he supposed, not a good sign. The Demerol would keep things smoothed for a few hours. Tomorrow he would drive down and see Doc Klein.

Larry came over and chose an alongside rocker. "Timmy really had a great time, Dog. I appreciate you taking him."

Old Dog rocked gently, feeling the first soothing of the Demerol. He coughed and cleared his throat before answering his brother.

"It was a great trip. Enjoyed seeing old friends, and Timmy was a pleasure. I think he had a good time."

"Timmy wore you out though, didn't he?"

Dog appeared a little surprised by the thought. "Not really, Larry. In fact, I probably took it easier because he was along. I slept while he went to the beach, and he sure didn't keep me up nights. We had a good time together."

"The leathers are something, too, Adam. Thank you for doing that for him."

"He's worth it, Larry. A good boy."

"What's the Jap bike for, Dog?"

"Just something to fool with. I won't have it long."

Larry could feel his brother fading, so he went home. Old Dog worked off his boots and stretched out on his sofa. His eyes were heavy. Great stuff, Demerol, although its effects were wearing off a lot sooner than they once had.

If he used the Yamaha at all, it would have to be soon, so he had told Larry more or less the truth.

Thebes Construction had a big hole dug up on Dynamite. They had taken out a thick blue-clay deposit and used it to seal a dam. The hole would be refilled with ungraded screenings from a Thebes topsoil operation. If he did use the rice burner in his half-formed scheme, that hole was where the Yamaha would go. Dog hoped the hole did not get filled before he was done with the motorcycle.

Chapter 15

"You leave a urine sample?" Kline asked.

"What choice did I have? That nurse of yours would have milked it out of me."

"Fine nurse. I'm going to take blood as well."

"Why don't you just send me over to a lab? That's what you do with everyone else."

"Because you'd just say, 'To hell with it,' and ride off. You've done that before, Dog."

"God, Doc, that was forty years ago, and there was a war on."

"They say you can't teach an old dog new tricks, Old Dog." Klein was obviously pleased with his cleverness. "Quiet, while I listen to your chest."

"Breathe in, breathe out, in, and out." The stethoscope touched coldly here and there.

"Breathing painful or hard? You short of breath?"

"All of the above, some of the time, anyway."

"You ought to hurt! Sounds like rocks rattling in a can. We ought to take X-rays."

"What the hell for, Doc? You know what's happening."

"Yeah, but you'll be asking 'How long've I got?' and you will expect me to know."

"How long've I got, Doc?"

"You're on schedule, Old Dog. I can clear up your lungs a little—not much." Klein appeared thoughtful. "I'm surprised you haven't more pain, Dog. Pleased, but surprised. You're down another three pounds. Guess you can tell your strength is failing."

"Yep. I'm grounding my Harley. I won't be riding anymore."

"About time. Going to Daytona wasn't too wise and getting caught in the rain was really dumb. You could still come down with pneumonia. Hell, you probably will, if you don't stay home and keep rested.

"You mean it might cut down my life span?"

"Not *might*—getting too worn out could end it."

"I've been getting an on and off ache across my lower back, Doc."

"Your urine may show something."

"Who cares what it shows? What'll stop it is what's important."

Klein extracted a pint bottle from a glass cabinet. He held it to the light. "This is the stuff, Dog. It's my improvement on an old elixir called Prompton's Cocktail. Prompton's is a mixture of powerful drugs meant to stop pain dead. This stuff," Klein shook his bottle suggestively, "will make gonads in a machinist's vise feel good."

"What's in it?"

Klein tried to look mysterious, "You don't want to know. Only thing I'll say is that you should be near a bed when you take it because you're not going far afterwards."

He glared accusingly at Old Dog. "For God's sake, don't take it and try driving, Dog. That would be deadly."

Old Dog took the bottle. "Maybe this would be the stuff I'll want . . . later on."

Klein sobered, "It would do, Dog, but don't hoard it now. I'll have what you need. I've already told you that."

Old Dog said, "You're a hell of a good friend, Doc. I'm grateful for all of this. Guess you know that."

"I know, Dog." The doctor slapped his patient's naked shoulder and glanced at the scar of the bullet's exit wound in Dog's back. "I did a damned good job on that, Dog. Almost unnoticeable."

"I've told you a dozen times, Doc, they cleaned it all up in Tokyo General. Hell, they thought our corpsman had sewed it together with commo wire."

Going home, on his way upriver, Old Dog drove out the Linglestown Road and turned left up the mountain. Another left took him back along the mountain toward the Susquehanna. Bat Stailey's house appeared on the right. He drove past, looking for life, but nothing stirred. He turned around and headed back; darned if a car wasn't pulling into the drive. It was not the limousine, but with the electric gate open, Old Dog could look in. The limo was parked within view. Bat was probably at home.

The last week of March was coming up, and Hunch would ride. What should he do about it? Old Dog rebalanced the question all the way to Duncannon.

Dog said, "I think I've got to tell Timmy straight out that I'm dying and won't be around much longer."

Old Dog's bluntness always jolted his brother. God, Dog spoke of dying as if it were taking a trip to Arizona or something. Still, Dog was right. It was time, and Larry was glad his brother would do the first explaining. It would not be easy, and Tim would suffer, but what better choice was there?

Larry said, "It is time, Adam. He knows you're bad sick and he wonders. When do you want to tell him?"

"Right now, I guess. Nothing like this gets easier to say."

"Want me to stay out here with you?"

"I don't think so, Larry. I don't want him having to keep up a front 'cause we're all looking at him."

Larry rose, wishing he had the will to say, "I'll tell him myself." Timmy was his son, but the reality was, Old Dog would do it better.

He said, "I'll send him out, Adam," and walked to the house a little less erect than usual.

Timmy barreled around the porch comer, obviously astride a 2000 or more cc Harley Davidson. "You wanted me, Uncle Dog?"

"Yep, come up here where we're eye-to-eye. I've got a job I need help on, but there's a thing or two you have to know first."

Tim leaped the steps and perched on a rocker half facing his uncle, his expression guilelessly hopeful. Old Dog hated wounding him.

"OK now, Tim, this is serious business, and the only way to tell it is to jump straight in and go for the far side, no easing up or veering off, and no later on stuff either. You agree?"

Of course he agreed.

Old Dog made his sigh deliberate and long. "You know I've been sick for a while now, right?"

He made a point of making his smile humorous. "If I lose any more weight I'll look like soda straw."

Dog did not linger. "The fact is, Tim, I've got cancer. I've got it bad, and I'm going to die from it." His nephew's face blanked, and Old Dog saw the boy's lip begin to quiver, so he pushed on.

"But, that isn't all bad, Tim. There is some good news. It looks as though I'm not going to have to do a lot of painful suffering, and I want you to know I feel real grateful for that."

Tim's eyes were awash, and he wrung his hands together.

"Now, this is a little hard for me to talk about, so what I would like you to do, Tim, is take a slow walk around behind the barn while I go inside, take a pill, and get my thoughts together, OK? Come on back when you think I'm ready."

Old Dog pretended the boy had answered. He went inside, and an instant later heard Tim dash down the steps and away. This was no motorcycle play; Timmy fled. Old Dog sighed in genuine regret. Dying wasn't hard, it was all the preliminaries that wore a man down.

Dog took his time, poking around inside, giving Tim room to gain control. Then he went onto the porch and eased back into his rocker. After a bit, Timmy reappeared, unsure of how to act, unaware of the dried tears on his cheeks.

Dog said, "Now, where was I? Oh yes, I was getting to the part where I need some help. I figure you and I can get this done together.

"What I'm going to do is put the old shovelhead into storage. The deal will be that it stays where we put it until you are eighteen—or older if your folks decide that is best. Then it will be yours.

"Storing is a problem. If we just lock the Harley up somewhere, as sure as I'm sitting here, it will have to be moved and probably it will get knocked around. So my plan is that we'll haul the bike up into the barn peak, right up to the ridge board. It'll be bone dry up there, the weight will be off the springs, and we will cover it up real well.

"I'll need you to do most of the heavy work, especially the up high part. Guess I could summon the strength, but I sure don't want to. You game for it?"

Tim nodded heavily, aware that Old Dog was trying to make things easier for him. Unable to hold it in, he burst out, "You can't just go and die, Uncle Dog—they must be able to do something." Tears flowed unrestrained.

Dog pursed his lips and pretended to consider.

"Well, Tim, I wish there were treatments that could do some good. Believe me, I've had the most famous doctors in the country working on it.

"The problem is the cancer is all through me. Cutting would just help spread the stuff. Using chemicals can't begin to get to the bad cells. The trouble there is that if you use chemicals strong enough to kill the cancer, the patient dies, too. Then there's radiation, but the same thing is true; they'd have to give me a week in a microwave oven to get 'em all.

"Nope, it's all been looked at, Tim. Only thing left to do is face up to it and enjoy whatever time is left."

Old Dog deliberately raised the time question because it too had to be dealt with.

"How long do you figure, Uncle Dog?" The jagged misery in the boy's voice cut deep.

"Oh, a few weeks yet. It'll be long enough, Tim. I've got a lot of odds and ends to clean up."

Old Dog got to the hardest part. "Now, there's one last thing about me dying that I want you to understand because it goes against what a lot of people think is right."

The Hemlock Society pointed out the importance of having the family know what was coming and to understand—whether they approved or not. Dog had the boy's attention so he went at it.

"If a man insists on suffering to the end, dying of cancer can be a horrible thing. The way I see it, modern medicine gets in the way of God's plan. The body keeps trying to die and doctoring keeps it alive. Even when it is so late the patient couldn't live a second without machines, we keep life signs blinking away. I've never thought that was sensible.

"Here's where the hard part comes in—not for me, you understand, but for some people.

"Right now, I'm alive and getting around because of powerful doctoring. Fair enough, and I'm grateful, but I'm stretching living out beyond what's natural.

"Let's just suppose that without pills and doctoring I would have died last month, which could have happened. If that's so, I've already lived longer than God had me figured for. A man can hang on too long, Tim. If I did that, toward the end I'd get disgusting to look at. I probably wouldn't know a hell of a lot, and just keeping my mostly dead old carcass breathing would take all kinds of time and money that could be used for better things.

"My plan is to stay on until it isn't fun anymore. When I get to hurting too much I'm going to use the same doctoring that kept me here to let myself go peacefully and with some dignity left."

Old Dog leaned a little forward, closer to his nephew, as if to confide secrets to him.

"I've been an independent and proud man most of my life, Timmy, riding free with the wind in my hair. Can you imagine how awful it would be for me to be laid out in a hospital with tubes and machines hooked into me, filled with pain or dope, wasted into a living skeleton, being treated like the tiniest baby in the world? And all the time I'd know I stunk of death and was pitied by everybody, without one single chance of getting an ounce better?

"If a guy could get well, all the ugly treatments might be worthwhile, but when you are already past your allotted time—if medicine had stayed out—and you can't ever recover anyway . . . it would be horrible for me to go through and just as bad for you and your mother and father to see."

Old Dog tried to wax enthusiastic. "I've got a better way, Timmy. What I'll do is this: I'll keep on until the misery gets too hard. Then, while I'm still able, I'll go alone to a place that's special to me. It's a long way from here. I'll take some powerful medicine I've got, and while it's working and before I drop off to sleep, I'll remember all the good things I've seen and done, especially you and your family. Then I'll just never wake up. That way, I won't be fighting God's wishes to some selfish and expensive bitter end. It'll be peaceful and easy with good thoughts. I'll even leave a map in case anybody needs to find my worthless old bones. Fact is, though, I'd just as soon be left out there where I'll become part of nature, instead of getting preserved and packed in a fancy box."

Old Dog figured he had talked his nephew past hysterics or over-long weeping. The boy would not want to remember himself that way. Men, it seemed, were supposed to keep stiff upper lips and carry on no matter how their hearts wept. Psychiatrists, feminists, and softer males claimed that was all wrong, and that men should release their emotions for the world to see. Dog personally doubted the wisdom of most men flaunting deepest feelings. It might get by in structured and sheltered societies, but where his bike had roamed, emotional displays had better be on the hard side. A man could rage, rip, and tear and remain respected. Weep, and a hardier type was likely to stomp on the weeper's face.

Perhaps men were knotted and warped by stifling tears and failing to holler "I'm sorry" every few hours, but Old Dog did not feel it, and he had not seen it. Dog expected his nephew hoped to be what he saw as manly, and memories of sobbing around when the going seemed tough would not help. A man trying to stand tall had it rough enough without recalling previous collapses—at any age.

In the morning they took the pickup over the mountain to Howell's Harley shop on the Carlisle Pike. Old Dog said it was important to store the bike with fresh oil in its belly. They would also buy new spark plugs and leave them in a saddlebag for when Tim put the old shovel back on the road. Old Dog had already signed over the notarized title and a request for a new one in Timothy Carlisle's name would eventually labor its way through Harrisburg's ossified governmental systems. Dog wryly suggested that by the time Tim got his paperwork he'd be of age to take the bike down.

Howell's lay on the south side of the pike. A paunchy looking rider was just crawling off a once fancy Harley, gone to ruin through neglect. They stopped to look, and Tim said, "Gee, all the chrome's rusted right through."

"Yep, when this bike was new it was a dream machine. Too late now. Polish every week, Tim, or a street bike will get away from you. That's one of the reasons we're storing your ride in a super-dry spot. Your tires will have to be replaced, of course. Never risk a bad tire. A blow out at any speed is something you never want to experience."

"You ever have one, Uncle Dog?"

"Never on the road. Had a rear tire go on a dirt flat track when I was young. No way to control upright. I laid her down and tried to kick clear before I got too tangled.

The track had a protective outside berm. I slid up it, doing pretty well with my leathers protecting, but still going fast. Went over the top and broke off an armload of dead pine branches about six feet in the air. Landed on pine needles and got up unhurt. Scared hell out of me, though. Tore up the bike, of course."

"Wow!"

"I don't recommend it."

They went in and poked through the Harley-Davidson T-shirts for a minute. Finding nothing inspirational, Tim went to check out the showroom bikes and Old Dog made his way to the service counter to line up beside the neglected bike's rider. Old Dog glanced over and his mind said, "Oh hell!" He looked away, but doubted it would do any good.

He felt the rider's eyes touch him—then examine closer. Studying me like a bug, Dog thought. Old Dog slid a hand into the side pocket of his jacket, avoiding eye contact, waiting it out.

When it came, the rider's voice was a snarl.

"I know you!"

Old Dog was studying literature scattered on the counter and ignored the speaker.

The rider kept on. "I mean you, old man."

The words dripped hatred.

Old Dog finally looked around. His eyes were cold, his voice disinterested. "And I know you, Hunch." Dog let it lay there.

Up close, Hunch looked older, a thick-bodied beefy man with a pugnacious look and mean, close-together eyes. He wore gauntleted riding gloves against the late March cold, and he chose to suggestively beat one clenched fist against the other palm, glaring in open hatred at Old Dog.

Rocking on his toes a little, Hunch almost spat, "I'll bet you remember me." His thick lips sneered, "Now you're nothing but a withered up *old man*."

Old Dog faced Hunch more squarely. Apparently undismayed by Hunch's animosity, Dog said, "Well, you're about the same." He pretended to look closely. "How's your head, Hunch. Looks a little out of shape to me."

Hunch seemed to swell all over. He said, "Damn you . . ."

The female clerk interrupted. "No trouble in here, guys. Take it someplace else." She called behind her for assistance.

Old Dog's voice stayed cold. "There won't be any trouble, will there, Hunch?" Dog's hand came from his jacket pocket, and Hunch saw the flash of the stainless steel derringer in Dog's hand.

Old Dog said softly, "It's a. 22 magnum, Hunch. It'll give you a bad bellyache."

Hunch came off his toes, his eyes suddenly wary.

Dog said, "I see you're still riding Bidwell's Harley, Hunch. I thought even a stupid thug like you would have gotten rid of it by now."

Hunch's eyes turned startled. His voice rattled with unexpected uncertainty. "That's been my bike for years. I'll keep it as long as I want."

Dog laid it out flat. "Bidwell has never been seen since he rode off with you, Hunch. You killed the kid and took his motorcycle. The brothers know it, and they'll get around to dealing with you."

His eyes plainly nervous, Hunch defended. "I bought that Harley. Paid Bidwell cash and my old ride. I . . ."

"No you didn't, Hunch. You sold your wreck to a rider named Bates who hails from Denver. You killed Bidwell and stole his machine. It's coming around, Hunch, and it'll get to you."

Hunch lacked a poker face. Old Dog watched astonishment change to chagrin and settle into anxiety.

Hunch said, "I don't give a damn what you think, *old man.* "He again made the words an insult. "If you didn't have that gun, I'd fix you right now."

"No you wouldn't, Hunch. You will always bring a knife to a gunfight. You're a loser, Hunch. You always will be, so don't come against me. I never lose to sleaze bags like you."

Hunch practiced control, "All right, you've got the gun, but I know you're around. You won't be hard to find, and I'll make it a point. One of these days you'll look up, and there I'll be. Then we'll see."

Hunch snatched his helmet from the counter and stomped to the door. He held there, hungry for the last word. "You'll see me again, old man, and it'll be the last time." The words dripped venom.

Old Dog stepped to the window and watched Hunch throw gravel getting away.

Dog nodded to himself, as though deciding something. He said only, "You can bet on it."

Just drawing close, Timmy thought his uncle sounded pleased about something.

Chapter 16

Storing the Harley took most of the afternoon. Old Dog supervised from a board pile, and Timmy did the work. He ran the motorcycle until it was hot, then drained the used oil. The empty tank and engine were flushed with kerosene. A quart of new Harley 60 weight oil was put in and the engine turned over a few times to circulate and recoat everything with clean oil.

With Old Dog directing, Tim loosened the push rods. He removed the spark plugs, threw them away, and squirted oil on top of the pistons. The cycle was rolled a little in gear until both pistons were high in their cylinders. The spark plug holes were sealed with common cork bottle stoppers.

Tim disconnected the gas line from the carburetor and plugged it. He filled the fuel tanks to their brims. The gasoline would spoil, but it would keep the tanks from rusting. The battery was removed and set aside. Dog had a friend who could use it.

Old Dog had thick nylon straps to hold the motorcycle.

"How strong are these, Uncle Dog? We wouldn't want the bike to get loose."

"Each will safely lift two tons, Tim, and nylon won't rot or rust. As long as the sun doesn't beat on it, it'll stay as strong as new."

The straps were led under the motorcycle, and the loops brought together on top. A cable lift from an old trailer was still pulleyed to the barn's ridge board. A remnant from farming times, it could lift anything.

Old Dog had a number of worn bed sheets ready. Timmy draped them over the motorcycle, thoroughly concealing it. At his uncle's direction, he cranked the Harley five feet high. They stood back and watched as its swing slowed.

"Balances good, Uncle Dog."

"Yep, now gather those sheet ends into a bunch underneath, and I'll bind 'em tight with cord. A bed sheet is good covering. It will protect, and air gets through. Never use plastic. You'll get moisture, and that will mean rust."

The motorcycle rose ghost-like, the winch's steady clacking measuring its ascent.

Larry came out to watch.

"Ought to be safe up there, Dog."

"Safe enough. Just make sure he's ready for it before you bring the bike down. Young riders get hurt most often, Larry."

"Not before he's eighteen, Adam. We'll see that he goes to motorcycle school as well."

"That's wise."

Old Dog turned ironic. "Don't know that I've left the best of legacies, Larry. I've never claimed motorcycle riding was smart."

"Not much chance he won't ride, Dog. You've put that in him—for better or for worse. It'll be our job to see that he starts right."

"I'll miss seeing it, brother. The worst part of dying is realizing you aren't going to know how things turn out."

Tim and Larry placed the long ladder against the peak-trapped Harley, and Dog handed over a length of half inch braided nylon rope. "OK, Tim, each loop of this rope will hold six thousand pounds. You take at least four turns around the ridge pole and through the sling loops. Cinch 'em up good and tie off with a square knot. Then put a half hitch in each line end, so the knot can't work over the years." Tim climbed without hesitation.

Larry said, "His mother's scared of heights. I'm glad he didn't inherit that."

"Timmy's gutsy, Larry. Just like you were."

"Yeah, I made the teams by struggling at it till I finally got good enough. Tim has some of that. He's able to stick with his weightlifting, which is pretty boring, and he's been talking about shooting baskets like you said Harvey Thebes did. I think he'll set himself a schedule and go at it

"I see a lot of you in him though, Adam. He moves smooth and easy, like you did when we were young. Man, you had the moves."

"Wonder where they went? I haven't seen any in a long time."

Larry chuckled, "Know what you mean, Adam, but you've still got moves. Doc Klein says anybody but you would be in bed by now. Adam, your joints don't crack when you bend. You ever notice that? Getting up, the rest of us sound like breakfast cereal. Heck, you've still got oil in your joints."

Timmy hollered, "It's tight, Uncle Dog."

"OK, get a good grip, your Dad'll let off the cable, and there will be some slack."

The cable loosened, and the Harley came down a few inches. "We'll leave the cable in place, and it'll be there when the time comes to lower the bike."

Old Dog said, "Come on down," and Timmy braced his insteps against the ladder's uprights and slid down like a hurried fireman.

The ladder was laid aside, and the trio surveyed their work.

"Think it's safe up there, Uncle Dog?"

"Unless the barn burns."

"Oh man. I didn't think of that."

When he was alone, Old Dog dug through the barn's accumulated junk until he found a roll of brown coated wire. Produced for the military, the steel wire had almost no stretch. It was flexible and camouflage painted. The army had used it for booby trap tripwire. Larry had picked up the roll decades before when he had done a National Guard hitch. Old Dog had use for it.

Two hours before dark, Old Dog parked his truck and walked the half mile along the mountain to his lookout above Bat Stailey's backyard. No one splashed in the heated pool, but music could be heard through opened French doors. The night was again unseasonably warm, but Old Dog kept his gloves on.

Dog sat a while. Even the slow walking exhausted his lungs and trembled his legs. Once, well, once he could have run the distance without drawing a deep breath.

Where had it all gone? His body was becoming an embarrassment. Dog studied his exposed wrists, leaned down, showing bones and tendons. The skin was limp. He pinched some into a ridge. Elasticity gone, the ridge stayed there. Tired skin, tireder muscle, and probably brittle bones, Dog thought. He gave thanks that his mind was staying clear . . . or was it? What he intended to do damned sure wasn't what most would consider rational.

He planned to kill Hunch Watson—if that was Hunch's real name. He could couch it in no easier words. Taking out, wasting, doing in were handy conscience easers, but they were evasions. Old Dog would do what society should but never would accomplish—punish a murderer.

Hunch's own promises of vengeance made it all easier. It was likely that Hunch would eventually locate his old enemy, or at lest where he had lived before . . . but Old Dog did not seek self-defense justification. Hunch needed killing. He, Dog Carlisle, was the only tool available. Vengeance is mine, sayeth Old Dog.

Hell, slews of people did not believe a death penalty was moral under any circumstances, and here he was about to act as judge and executioner. Old Dog examined his conscience and discovered no qualms. It would be nice if there were others to do the job, to share responsibility, but there were none. Despite his claims to Hunch, no biking brothers would bring Hunch to account. Those were at best wishful words. Hunch would get off scot free unless . . .

Old Dog recognized that if he were not dying he too would let Hunch live. He might—probably would—pound Hunch senseless, but Hunch would, in the end, ride away. The risks of discovery and imprisonment were too great. The living had too much to lose to risk murder. Others might also beat the hell out of Hunch, and the biker community would certainly ostracize him, but kill him, fully avenge the young rider? Improbable.

None of that genuinely bothered Old Dog. He intended to go ahead. He wanted to be the one to rid the world of Hunch Watson.

And maybe, just maybe, Hunch might hold the key to at least locking away Bat Stailey, and that would be a worthwhile accomplishment.

One thing did bother Old Dog. He would like to face Hunch man-to-man. He would like to fight Hunch to the death—any weapon would do. But, he could not. He was old, sick, weak, and slow. Hunch would win. So, he had to go another, just as effective if less satisfying, route.

Dog rose and made his way through the woods to where Hunch would park his motorcycle. Hunch always used the same final one hundred yard plunge down the mountain, braked hard, and stepped off. He would surely take the same approach this time. Old Dog listened to the woods. Hunch's Jap bike was almost silenced. If Hunch was coming there would be only little warning, but Dog was intentionally early. Hunch had always come at dusk. There was plenty of time.

Old Dog walked fifty feet up Hunch's approach. Too close, he went another fifty. About right.

He unrolled his tripwire, careful to avoid crimping. He stretched it shoulder high and bow-string tight across the path. Against the backdrop of trees the coated steel wire was invisible.

Hunch would barrel downhill. He would be riding erect, looking ahead, preparing to stop. Dog had the wire a touch low, where it was sure to go under Hunch's chin.

Some called it clotheslining. It was vicious and certain. It was a weapon of war. The result would be instant and terminal. Old Dog hoped the motorcycle's crash would not carry to Bat Stailey's house. It was only a long stone's throw below.

Hunch did not come. When it was dark, Old Dog removed his wire. He would return. Hunch had always appeared during a month's last week. Dog hoped Hunch would not skip this visit. He also hoped his strength would hold up. God, he felt like crawling into the woods like a dying animal.

Not yet, tasks to accomplish first. Adam Carlisle was creating his personal monument, his anonymous gift to uncaring humanity's welfare.

On the third night, Stailey's right hand thug became restless. The burly head knocker named Clout repeatedly approached the screened door, looking expectantly into the woods behind the house. Old Dog said, "Ah hah," softly so only he could hear. He left his lookout and walked back to his tautly stretched wire. He again sat, this time out of sight, just above the wire, where a riderless motorcycle could not somehow find him.

The wait drew long, but Hunch was due. Stailey's man proved it. Old Dog felt no impatience. He wished there was a way he could let Hunch know he was about to receive justice, but that was impossible.

Well, little was perfect. It was more important that the wire clothesline do its job properly. If it did not . . . in his pocket, Dog's gloved hand gripped his tiny five-shot pistol.

Hunch was a little late. He could not safely ride the mountain after dark, so this evening he would have to hurry.

Old Dog heard the motorcycle first as a soft purr, seeming to drift directionless along the mountain. So quieted was the engine that its sound came only moments before it burst into view.

Hunch rode swiftly, twisting his machine expertly through the trees, familiar enough with the mountain to know his way. Old Dog saw the flash of his paint only an instant before the Kawasaki reached the open downslope—and the waiting wire.

For another instant before the downhill slope smoothed, Hunch and cycle were airborne, and Hunch actually opened the throttle for his closing dash.

Old Dog could hardly watch. What was about to happen was a biker's worst nightmare. A necktie of wire held no mercy, except being ultimately swift and final.

Hunch was sitting straight, focusing forward.

The motorcycle hurtled ahead, and then, as though reaching the end of a tether, Hunch stopped and was momentarily suspended. The wire twanged and snapped under the horrendous strain. It whipped itself into wraps around the floating figure before gravity took hold and Hunch's body slammed leadenly to the earth.

There was a tremendous spurt of blood, black in the forest's dim light, a geyser of death that shot from beneath Hunch's helmet. Old Dog had seen worse, but it could never be ignored, and he looked away.

Like a runaway freight, Hunch's machine plunged onward. It crashed against a smaller tree, somehow righted, and disappeared down the hill. An instant later Dog saw it bouncing sideward into a smashing roll that seemed to go on forever before he heard it come to a sliding stop. Dog wondered if the damned thing had reached the swimming pool.

He took a quick look at the downed rider. Hunch was done. The violent garroting had killed. The massive hemorrhage from severed arteries had only made sure. Old Dog experienced no regrets. As it had been in Korea long ago, enemy dead held no significance and little interest to the living. Dog headed downhill. What he needed next should be in Hunch's saddlebags.

The Kawasaki had gone a long way. It should not have. The bike should have immediately fallen on its side, slammed into trees and stalled. When Old Dog reached the battered motorcycle it was on its side and still running, the rear wheel, bent and twisted, but turning. Incredible! Dog reached for the kill button ... and Clout charged from the downhill woods only a few yards away.

Astonishment was mutual. Clout had no reason to expect anyone but Hunch to be at the motorcycle wreck, but here was a stranger bending over Hunch's smashed machine, perhaps reaching for Hunch's package. Clout reached for his pistol.

The crash had been loud enough to rouse the dead, but Old Dog had expected to have a little time. Clout appeared seemingly from nowhere. Dog saw Clout's hand go inside his coat, and Dog reached, too. He also dove for cover. There were large trees nearby, but Old Dog was more interested in the closest.

Clout was way ahead, and he did not wait. His pistol cracked a trio of hasty shots directed toward Old Dog's diving body. Whatever the saddlebags held was clearly worth killing for.

Old Dog hit and rolled, long unpracticed combat skills coming into play. His tiny pistol finally came free, but it was clumsy in his gloved hand. A fourth bullet chewed earth at his ear, disclosing the meager protection offered by his tree. Dog heard the gunman's feet, moving to get a better shot, Old Dog figured.

Dog cocked the pistol's hammer, gathered his nerve, and stuck the gun and his head around the tree trunk. Clout was in the open and moving, for the instant glancing down at his footing. No shots had come his way, he might have believed his opponent unarmed.

Old Dog's front sight was only decoration. There was no rear sight. The derringer was meant for close-in, belly-touching work, but if held rock solid it would shoot. Dog aimed at the middle of Clout's body. He held like iron, letting his target blur, concentrating on aligning the single sight atop the pistol's backstrap. He was only vaguely aware of Clout's own hasty reaction and their shots blended.

Bark splinters plucked at Dog's shoulder, but he ignored the distraction. Clout had frozen in place, his pistol still extended, but studying his free hand that moved hesitantly to his body. Old Dog recocked and concentrated on placing his front sight just beneath the gunman's chin. His tiny pistol popped again, its report sounding puny and ineffective.

Clout staggered. Hit again, Old Dog expected. Clout cursed with vicious intensity. His gun steadied and erupted in a hail of bullets. Dirt flew and wood chips fell. Through the intimidating barrage, Old Dog fought to resight and get off a third shot.

When would it end? Clout's pistol seemed to have a bottomless magazine.

Finally Clout's fire ceased. Believing himself untouched, Old Dog squeezed again, and Clout flinched for the third time.

Clout lowered his pistol, seemingly undecided on what to do. They were close, perhaps ten yards apart. Old Dog hoped the thug did not charge. A wrestling match would surely go to Stailey's man.

Dog dumped his fourth. 22 magnum round into Clout's middle, wondering if he was doing any good and whether he should hold his last cartridge for nose to nose work or shoot now while he had a motionless target.

The man was still erect but acting confused. Old Dog scrambled to his feet, and Clout raised his empty pistol as though to shoot. Dog knew it was unloaded because the slide was locked back denoting an empty magazine.

His derringer aimed, Dog stepped nearer. Every foot closer improved his chances of hitting a vital spot.

Clout fell! He sagged to his knees, features unresponsive. His pistol's muzzle dug into the forest floor, and his finger jerked the empty gun's trigger.

Clout sat heavily back on his heels. His mouth fell open and his tongue protruded. Limp and silent, Clout slumped onto his side, his pistol falling from a suddenly nerveless hand.

Old Dog stood over the body. It was a body. Dog remembered the look. He saw no blood. The .22 magnums left no gaping entrance wounds. He doubted any had exited, but at least one had punctured something big inside Clout. A heart shot or a blown aorta could kill like this.

Old Dog did not check his group. He had been lucky as much as skilled. If the gunman had taken time to aim, it would almost certainly have been Clout looking down on Adam Carlisle's dead carcass.

Clout had shot and hoped. Men armed with large capacity, semi-automatic pistols did a lot of that. A single, well aimed bullet beat the hell out of fourteen or so jerked off "Hail Mary" shots, but the temptation to pour it on usually overcame the will and concentration required to aim carefully and shoot exactly. Old Dog was thankful Clout had never learned.

Dog shut down the still running Kawasaki and knelt to open a saddlebag. Clout's sightless eyes stared at him, but Dog Carlisle had been examined by the dead before. He knew they never interfered.

God, he hurt all over. His hands shook. His breathing was wretched, and he had to delay while he fumbled a Doc Klein inhaler from a pocket. Proventil—it opened tubes and let in air.

Simple leaping and rolling had exhausted him more than a mile race would have in his youth, but he had managed it.

In fact, Clout's attack and subsequent demise might add substance to his plan for jailing Bat Stailey.

Old Dog paid attention to possible approach. He wondered if his hearing was going. Hunch's cycle had been almost on him before he heard it, and he had not detected the thug's rush at all. If Clout had heard the motorcycle crash, anyone else in the house would surely have noticed the shooting. They could be coming.

He got the saddlebag open. There was a wrapped package, tightly compressed, as stiff as a book. Dog stabbed his pistol's muzzle through the plastic wrap. Marijuana! Good! His plan could still work out

To reach the second saddlebag, Dog had to flip the motorcycle. It was already partway over. He heaved with his puny strength, and the bike crashed over and slid away. A hell of a racket, but no one had come yet.

The packet from the second bag was more limp, but Old Dog did not have to wonder. It was money, as sure as he handled it. How much? This was not the time for counting, but enough to make the late head-knocker Clout start shooting for it.

Old Dog stuffed the money pack into his shirt front where it bulged like a concealed law book. He wondered idly if it would stop a bullet.

Despite Clout's unexpected arrival, Old Dog thought his plan for Bat Stailey still had a chance. That no one had investigated the shooting should indicate that the Stailey house was now unoccupied. Clout could have been left to meet Hunch's drop-off while Stailey and company went elsewhere. Old Dog hoped it was so.

To win, Dog had to again risk. His intention had been to plant Hunch's marijuana, if the late unlamented had any, in one of the lockers around Stailey's pool. Dog would then call 911 and anonymously report that Bat Stailey had just killed a biker, and that he had dope hidden at his swimming pool. The resulting furor could have jailed Stailey, but with Clout down, and the house possibly empty, Old Dog believed he could do better. Dog wanted to get into Bat Stailey's house.

His shaky legs took him downhill to the low stone wall bordering Stailey's pool. All was still. One screened door hung open, evidence of Clout's hurried investigation of the motorcycle crash.

Dog crossed the wall quickly and rounded the swimming pool. His pistol with its single remaining round held out of sight, he stuck his head inside the house. No one. Hot damn, he would go for it.

Old Dog gave the luxurious home a rapid walk through. Handsome, no question about it, deep rugs and rich furnishings. He looked into the front yard. Empty.

Stailey's bedroom would be the place. Dog found it on the second floor. Where to hide the dope? The money, of course, would go with him to Perry County.

There was luggage in a closet. Good enough, Stailey's personal suitcase ought to tie in nicely. He selected a smaller Samsonite that had stickers and showed use. There were odds and ends of clothing inside. The marijuana fit neatly.

Old Dog delayed his departure, wishing he could better set the scene. He smiled grimly, deciding to risk a clincher.

He had owned the .22 magnum derringer for a dozen years. He had picked it up at a yard sale in Indiana. The pistol could not be traced to him. Dog sat on Stailey's bed and pulled the pistol apart. There were only three pieces and the five cartridges. Using a corner of Stailey's bed sheet, he wiped clean the cartridge cases and replaced them in the cylinder. He wiped down the outside of the pistol so no fingerprints could remain there. The fouled bore and cylinder face would prove recent firing. The bullets in Clout's body would match any fired through the pistol. Old Dog's teeth showed. Get out of this one, Stailey.

When the police came, they would not miss the opportunity to legally search Stailey's home. The law wanted Bat, and who could tell what a diligent search might turn up. The search would be hungry and thorough. Top on their list would be the gun that shot Clout to death, and they would find it.

Not under Stailey's mattress or pillow. Even in haste, Stailey would not be that stupid. Old Dog went to the closet. An old bathrobe hung back among sport coats. Detectives would search every garment. Dog reached in and tried to jam the pistol into the furthest pocket. It snagged. Old Dog checked to see why. His searching fingers found a folded flat packet of bills. A quick thumb through showed all hundreds. This time Dog laughed aloud, Perry County luck—it really existed. He replaced the money with the pistol. When a gun turned up instead of his cash, Stailey would have to believe an inside job. Who would he suspect? Everyone probably, but howl frame-up as loud as he might, police would be hard to convince.

Old Dog moved downstairs and chose a chair that looked out the front window. He poured himself a glass of milk from Stailey's refrigerator and sat down to count money and wait.

Thirty thousand dollars! Whew! Significant money to any honest man. Dog wondered who handed the funds to Hunch the courier. Each and every month? Big money was changing hands. Perhaps the money was only chicken feed to Stailey, skimmings from one or another nefarious activity. Well, this particular bundle Stailey would never see. Dog returned the package to the safety of his shirt.

Before his milk was gone, the electric gate began to open, and Old Dog could see the limo waiting to enter. He hurried to the kitchen, quickly rinsed his glass and put it away. He snatched the kitchen phone. It was cordless, and he carried it out the pool door. Beyond the stone wall, where he had woods cover, he dialed 911. The answer was immediate.

Old Dog put panic into his voice. "He killed 'em both. Bat Stailey strangled the biker and shot the other guy with a pistol."

"May I have your name, sir?"

"Like hell, I'm gettin' the hell out of here. Both of 'em are layin' dead in the woods behind Stailey's house. I seen . . ."

"Sir, can you take it more slowly?"

"Slowly, hell, you don't believe me, you look in the wood's behind Stailey's pool. Both guys are layin' there. Hell, Stailey took one's head near off, and he shot the other guy in the guts about ten times."

"Sir . . . "

"Oh man, here he comes again. I'm out of here." Old Dog shut down.

A voice called from inside. "Clout, hey Clout?" A head peered outside, then disappeared. "He isn't out there, Mister Stailey."

Old Dog flipped the phone into the middle of Stailey's pool. It sank as he began feeling his way through the dark woods.

The homicide Lieutenant said, "It sounds like someone's having fun. I'd like to catch the bastard."

"Yeah, it'd be a cold day in hell when Bat Stailey pulled a trigger himself."

"Wouldn't it be nice, though?"

The Lieutenant sighed in disgust. "Well, we've got to take a look. Can't just ignore it"

A patrolman rose. "I'll take it, Lieutenant. I'm going out to Dauphin anyway. I'll poke through the woods without disturbing citizen Stailey."

"Yeah, don't stir up anything. His attorney would be on the line before you could radio in."

"I'll call when I find the bodies. ""

They laughed together. "Fine, I'll wait anxiously."

Old Dog could not hurry. He was too bushed. In the dark, the half mile of woods took forever. At the truck he sucked on the inhaler and decided he would have to swallow a pain pill. A pair of codeine would lighten his backache, and codeine did not make him sleepy, the way morphine did.

It felt good sitting in the truck cab, the night quiet around him. It was nice having his gloves off. He had worn them constantly, so no Carlisle fingerprints could show on anything. Modern forensic techniques could disclose all kinds of secrets so he planned on dumping his gloves and his boots. He had others that would not reveal gunpowder or recognizable sole prints. The remainder of the tripwire roll was long gone in the garbage. He could think of only one more precaution.

The codeine began to take hold, and although it induced a touch of lassitude, Dog thought it time to go. There was only one way out, back past Stailey's house. He doubted investigators would yet be taking passing vehicle numbers. He doubted they ever would. Bat Stailey was neatly boxed. The police would not look further.

The patrolman's voice was shocked.

"Lieutenant, they're there! The bodies are there, and Stailey is in the house. I saw him."

The Lieutenant's chair straightened with a crash. "Holy hell! You're sure?"

"Lieutenant . . ."

"All right! Where are you, now?"

"I'm using a fast-food phone. I didn't want this on the air."

"Good move. You get back. Sit on the crime scene. We'll come with everything."

The Lieutenant hung up and stood for an instant, still hardly believing. He said again, "Holy hell!" Then got busy.

With the codeine working, Old Dog felt up to one more move. He drove through Duncannon and took the back road toward Bloomfield. He passed Aqueduct and Delancy's old antique shop. Before Pine Grove he turned onto a side road. Later he turned up a lane and pushed in alongside an old farm house.

Tom Bell dealt in everything legal. He sold antiques, books, and paintings. You could buy a motorcycle from Tom, and he might have a Corvette on hand. Bell was also a gun and knife trader.

Bell said, "Hell, Dog, I'm heading for Florida in two hours. Everything I own is packed."

Dog said, "You'd need six semi-trailers to move the top layer, Bell. What I want is small, anyway."

"What'd that be?"

"You've got a couple of those five-shot derringers they make out in Utah, right?"

"I've got one or two. What kind do you want?"

"A .22 magnum."

"I've got one. Like new. Cost you one hundred and fifty."

"Tom . . ."

"Well, how much do you figure it's worth?"

"A hundred to a friend."

"We'll split. One hundred and twenty-five."

"Sold."

Bell grumbled, "I ought to get ten dollars for digging it out." His van was full.

"You're going south?"

"Yep, I'm going to hit the knife shows for a month. I'll be back in May or maybe June."

"You'll miss the spring auctions, man."

"Can't buy anything at auction anymore, anyway."

Bell produced the pistol. As far as Dog could tell it was identical to his own.

"Where'd you get this gun?"

"How in hell would I remember? They come and they go. Down south somewhere, I suppose."

"You got any cartridges?"

"I got some in the house, but they're old."

"I only want five. An empty gun isn't much use."

"That kind of gun isn't much use anytime."

"I like it."

Old Dog dropped the pistol into his pocket. It felt natural. He was pleased that Bell's cartridges were a different brand than his own had been. Every bit of cover could help—if anyone ever came looking.

Tom Bell headed for Florida. Old Dog went home. By the time Bell got back, the Bat Stailey killings would be old hat—not that a trader like Bell would remember peddling the gun anyway. Too many items came and went to recall a lone pistol sale. It was perfect.

Chapter 17

It was nearly noon before Larry Carlisle saw Old Dog settle into a porch rocker. A warming sun struck the front of Dog's shanty further heating the dregs of another unseasonably warm night.

Many wondered at the consistency of the season's high temperatures, and although reassured by TV weathermen that hot spring weather was not unprecedented, some believed the long predicted greenhouse effect was now measurable. If spring was like summer, what would July and August be like?

Larry said, "Dog's finally up, Arlis. I'm going over and tell him the news."

His wife crossed her kitchen to look out her back window. "Adam hasn't gotten dressed. That's a first, Larry. He is not feeling good." Despite her attempt to sound disinterested, Larry could hear concern in her voice.

Old Dog, with his outwardly carefree ways, challenged almost everything Arlis believed important. His wife might sniff and hotly deny it, but she still had a spot in her heart for her adventuring, good-for-nothing, roamer-of-a-wastrel brother-in-law.

Arlis had used those descriptions and harsher ones over the years, but the words only demonstrated her exasperation. If asked, Arlis Carlisle would likely deny giving a serious hoot about Old Dog, but Larry knew better. Perhaps she exclaimed too often or too loudly. Arlis too was pained by Dog's rapid decline.

As if reading her husband's thoughts, Arlis said, "He ought to be in a hospital where he could be taken care of."

Larry noted she did not suggest moving Old Dog into their home. His wife's concern would not extend that far.

"We'll keep an eye on him." Larry hesitated then decided to go ahead.

"You do understand what Dog intends doing, don't you, Arlis?"

"Of course I do. He's been talking about it for years, hasn't he?"

"Yes, he has. He wanted us to know that he was serious."

"Well, it's wrong. Suicide is against God's will. It's unchristian."

Larry rarely opposed his wife's views. Unless they caused difficulty, he was inclined to let Arlis's stern opinions float unacknowledged.

At the moment, equally disturbed by Old Dog's illness, he chose to respond.

"Adam's thought it through a thousand times, Arlis. He is at peace with himself, and it seems to me we should be thankful for him. A lot of folks will go to their maker more uncertain than Old Dog."

"The Bible says . . ."

"Dang it, I know what the Bible says. It happens that Adam doesn't agree. It isn't our business to force our beliefs on him. Dog made up his mind years ago. He has never faltered. If he got terminal and was suffering, the way so many people we know have suffered, he would end his own life. Not in some disgusting way like shooting his head off or hanging himself in the barn, but going peaceful and with dignity. 'Sailing away with class,' he likes to say.

"Darn it, Arlis. Old Dog's self-deliverance takes at least as much courage as it does to lay around a hospital all doped up, just hanging on till the end. Most people haven't got the heart to do what they would actually prefer, so they suffer out their time. That's the difference between Adam's way and the usual."

Larry hesitated only an instant before adding, "I think Adam also expects to save us a lot of suffering and pointless expense. We ought to keep that in mind when we are criticizing him."

"It still isn't right, and we ought to have the minister out here to talk to him."

Larry snorted. "Old Dog would eat the man alive. My Lord, Arlis, Adam has been polishing his arguments for decades. He would quote scripture that the reverend might never have examined. Dog would use a dozen different religions for support and about a hundred philosophical opinions. He would list legal precedents and . . . why on earth would you want to shove our pastor into that buzzsaw?"

His wife clattered dishes angrily. She had no arguable position. She just knew it was wrong, just like everybody else knew killing yourself was terrible. She shuddered in revulsion.

Larry said, "I'm going over and tell him about the TV."

"Well, see if he would like some nice vegetable soup. It might make him feel stronger."

"I'll ask, but all he gets down are milkshakes, says they'll keep him going . . . long enough."

Old Dog was still groggy from Doc Klein's elixer. When he had come home, he had hit it hard, pleased to be knocked out while the authorities worked out the unexpected exposure of Bat Stailey.

Wrapped in his robe and a fluffy king-size blanket, Dog was content to porch sit and ponder his timing. He had awakened with a deep, lung-ripping cough that took a lot of inhaler pumping to subdue. He choked up matter and, when he looked, blood specks were plain to see. They had not appeared before. Time was marching on, and he did not wish to discover it was later than he thought.

What a farce it would be after all his talk to keel over and wake up pinned to a hospital bed until he died. What a bummer! It was about time to make his move.

He was still surprisingly mobile. He had hiked and hustled around pretty vigorously last night. For a moment he saw again Hunch's midair halt and Clout's slow sag and still twitching finger on his empty pistol's trigger.

The remembering was neither pleasant nor morbid. Old Dog supposed he must be coarse and calloused to remain un-traumatized after killing two human beings, but he expected the world really was a better place without Hunch and Clout. He had cleared garbage from the path of human progress, and he suffered no remorse.

Of course, jailing Bat Stailey had been the bigger victory. Authorities were waiting for their shot at Bat, and they would not miss their chance. They would prosecute with fervor. By the time Stailey got out of prison he would be old and out of action. Not quite as satisfying as shooting him dead, but good enough. Old Dog wondered how many bodies the racketeer had caused to be buried and how many lives he had destroyed through his promotion of about every human vice known. Probably about as many as putting Stailey away would save. The concept was a comfortable equation.

Bat Stailey could not have attained his eminence in gangland hierarchy without making his own bones. Somewhere, back along Stailey's criminal trail, moldered the remains of those he had murdered for gain. The law knew it. Some of the public recognized the certainty of the elegant Don's violently criminal road, but the evidence would never be forthcoming. Crime bosses like Bat Stailey were armored by layers of fellow conspirators. Hit men eliminated witnesses, and clever lawyers out-papered underpaid and understaffed, inexperienced prosecutors. The Staileys of organized crime were rarely pulled down.

But, Old Dog Carlisle had gotten the bastard! Dog rocked in some contentment. Only he would ever know, unless . . . Dog gave thought to certain improbabilities.

Larry came over excited. He started talking before he reached the first step.

"You see the news, Dog?"

Larry did not wait for an answer. "A little was on the eight o'clock news, but your light was out so I figure you missed it.

"There was good coverage this morning. Timmy wanted to wake you up, but I got him off to school.

"Bat Stailey's been arrested for murder, and it looks like they've got him cold. They even showed the gun on TV. Stailey strangled one guy, they said, and shot another. There was dope, too. The DEA and maybe the FBI are in on it. They got in because of the dope and the strangled guy's motorcycle being registered out of state. Crossing state lines made it a federal rap, I guess.

Old Dog made his voice surprised. The pleasure was easy. "So they finally got Stailey. About time."

Larry said, "I'll move your TV out here, and we'll catch the noon news." He came back lugging the set, trailing cord and cable. He perched the TV where they could both see it.

"You want 8, 21, or 27?"

"Get 27. They've got a Perry County weatherman, and we ought to stay loyal."

They were early, so Larry muted the sound.

"Have a bad night, Adam?"

"Nope, had a great night. Doc Klein's secret potion put me out for hours." Dog chuckled, "I didn't know my bladder could last that long."

Larry examined his brother critically. "You going to see Doc again soon, Dog?"

There was worry in his brother's words, and Old Dog supposed he did look like some sort of road kill.

"Not much use, Larry. Doc's sending me up a big bottle of his good stuff. I'll take it with me when I go."

"God, Adam . . ."

"Come on, brother. Everybody gets his turn. If I could live, I would. Hell, Larry, in a way I'm having the best of it. I get to pick the way I die, where I choose to die, and, with some big limitations, exactly when."

"You could just stay here, Adam. You could be in the Bloomfield cemetery with the rest of our family. That's where we all should be."

Old Dog rocked, reviewing thoughts he had studied out years before.

"I could do that." He chuckled, "Though Arlis would prefer just rolling me down the bank into the ice pond."

"Oh, Adam . . ."

"But, I want to try one last adventure, Larry. I want to struggle and chew at one final sort of crazy goal that not a person in one hundred thousand would even consider. If I make it, I'll lay back and pass over feeling content with the life I had."

His brother smiled a little. "You make it sound so good I want to come along."

"Well, now that I'm this close, I'm sort of looking forward to it. It'll be tough, so I can't wait too long, but . . . OK, here's the news. Turn it up loud."

The segment was big time. CNN would make mention, and newspapers across the land might touch on Bat Stailey's arrest. Stailey was no John Gotti, but his name was known. The announcer put heart into his reading.

"In a stunning strike, Pennsylvania State Police, FBI, and DEA officers arrested Batey R. Stailey of RD Linglestown, charging him with the murder of two men. The bodies were . . ."

The visuals were damning. The eye of the camera did not blink. Hunch's body was mercifully covered, but a still of Clout, his empty pistol, slide locked open, near his hand was included. Officials with vests and jackets lettered Police, FBI, and DEA milled and were shown poking into things.

A large packet believed to be marijuana was displayed for the camera, and a photographer caught a clip of a heavy bellied detective carrying the alleged murder weapon clutched in surgical forceps.

Larry said, "Maybe they got his fingerprints on the gun. Maybe he had it in his pocket."

"I've read that despite crime novels, police don't often get prints off of guns."

"They've got him this time, Dog. No way he can slip out."

Larry startled Old Dog saying, "That'll teach him to beat up on a Perry County Carlisle."

"What?"

"I figure hammering on you turned his luck bad, Dog."

Dog's heart rate returned toward normal. "If that was it, brother, it sure worked slow. That whipping happened more than two years ago, and Stailey didn't do it himself."

"Doesn't matter, Dog. They've always said, 'Don't mess with a Perry Countian.'"

Old Dog asked, "Who says that, Larry?" His brother had given him a jolt with the punching-out connection. It would be best to play it on out until the fun was gone.

"I heard Grandpa say it."

"I never did."

"Grandpa was telling about some of the old settlers who were first into these mountains."

"It was part of Cumberland County back then."

"I know that, Dog. It's the idea that messing with people from up here got you hurt that counts."

"Stailey messed with a lot of people I imagine, only this time he got caught."

"Dumb thing for him to do."

"That'll probably be his defense."

"What do you mean?"

"Stailey will claim he is obviously too smart to have killed two people in his own yard, so he is a victim of some sort of setup."

"Nobody will buy that"

"You just said it was really dumb, brother. Others will agree, and Stailey will have the best attorneys."

Talking like that made Old Dog nervous. Stailey was slick. Could he get out of a net this tight?

Old Dog did not really see how.

Doc Klein brought his elixir in person. He pulled an immense Cadillac close to Old Dog's steps and climbed out, looking critically about.

Old Dog and Timmy were waiting for the six o'clock news. On this second day, Bat Stailey was still the big story.

Old Dog lowered his moccasin clad feet and rose with an audible grunt.

"Holy hell. Lay out a carpet. Doc Klein hasn't stepped off pavement in forty years."

Klein asked, "Where's your outhouse, Dog? It's a long trip up here."

"We don't have an outhouse, Doctor Klein. Uncle Dog's got real plumbing." Timmy was quick with his defense. "He's got a microwave and air conditioning. Uncle Dog's got everything a man needs."

Old Dog pointed inside, knowing Klein was already familiar with the place. They shook hands in passing, the doctor's eyes evaluating Dog's increasingly leaned frame and hollowed features.

"Take your time, Doc. We'll wait."

"At my age, everything takes time. Sit down before you collapse. You look awful."

Timmy said, "I don't think you look so bad, Uncle Dog."

"You don't? Well, I ought to look awful. I feel bad enough." Old Dog's slap on his nephew's shoulder belied the harshness of his words.

Klein returned and chose a seat. "Get the package off the seat, will you, Tim? It's for your uncle."

"Doc, that's the biggest, ugliest automobile I've ever seen. Fins? It must be fifty years old." Old Dog's tone was disdainful.

Klein sounded proud. He savored his description. "That's a 1956 Caddie, Dog. A gen-u-wine classic. Nobody makes 'em like that anymore."

"Thank heaven. It ever get past a gas station without stopping?"

"Burns a little, but hell, Dog, gas is cheaper now, compared to income, than it's ever been."

"Compared to whose income? You're not politically correct on this one, Doc."

"When have I ever been?"

They rumbled appreciatively.

"So, how are you doing, Dog?"

"A lot of notches on my short timer's stick, Doc."

Klein remembered rear echelon types almost ready to leave Korea walking around showing their short timer sticks with carved-in notches counting the days before rotation to the States. He expected Old Dog was about through his tour.

"Much pain?"

"A hell of a lot sometimes, but I'll stick around a while yet"

"Cramps?"

"Those, too, mostly in my legs. In my gut sometimes."

"Don't let it catch you, Dog. A man can get awful close to going down without realizing it"

"I'm watching. Funny thing is, I can still get around some if I grit my teeth and go at it"

"You still living on milkshakes?"

"Chocolate shakes, Doc. Other flavors don't set as well."

"I'll get you in the medical journals under Miracle Diet."

"Want a shake now, Uncle Dog?" Timmy was ready.

"Yeah, that'd be fine, Tim. You want a shake, Doc?"

"God no, they're full of cholesterol."

Tim sped inside. Klein added, "Timmy seems to be taking it well."

"Yeah, he's doing good. Hauling it out in the open and being willing to talk about it gets everyone relaxed and more natural."

Old Dog grinned, "Except Arlis. She gets all shook, so when she comes around I talk about rotting away and my guts being eaten alive by raging cancer cells that look like miniature maggots. Gets her every time."

Klein groaned. "You're a trial, Old Dog."

Dog grinned, "It's my duty, Doc."

The news came on, and Old Dog turned up the volume. "I can't wait to hear the Bat Stailey part, Doc. A couple of his thugs beat hell out of me a few years back. In fact, I'm sticking around in part to see Stailey take his fall."

Unbelievable! A man had come forward and admitted to the killings, including planting the dope and the pistol. All done before Bat Stailey had come home, he claimed.

Old Dog set his shake aside, untasted.

The confession had been distributed on videotape to the TV stations. The police and federal authorities got the news secondhand. The apparent murderer turned himself in to a TV reporter.

Old Dog said, "Isn't that hell?"

Larry came running over from his house. "Can you believe that, Dog? Hi Doc. That Louseball Stailey has done it again. He's home free."

Klein asked, "Why are you surprised? Stailey's people are probably squeezing the guy's father's head or maybe they are paying for his wife's heart-lung transplant."

Larry claimed, "Well, the cops will tell if the bum confessing is lying. There will be stuff he doesn't know. "

Old Dog roused to say, "He'll claim he was on dope and can't remember a lot of things. His lawyers—I'll bet they are big, important guys—will refuse to let him say more."

Doc Klein added, "They'll plead that the dead guys were rats that deserved what they got. Hell, the jury will probably agree. The guy will do a couple of years and come out with big bucks in a foreign bank."

Old Dog said, "God!"

Larry had an offering. "How about this: Clout garroted the dead biker and opened up with his pistol on the confessee. So, the confessee killed him in self-defense and, hating Bat Stailey, he planted the pistol and the biker's dope in Stailey's house. He called in and then ran for it—but of course his conscience rose and he had to confess . . . because it was the right thing to do."

Doc Klein said, "By gosh, I believe that's what really happened. I see it now. The poor guy . . . and poor innocent Mister Batey Stailey."

Old Dog had nothing to say. He picked up his shake and sipped at it, his eyes distant, as if he were thinking.

Chapter 18

Timmy was in school, Larry was visiting customers, and Arlis had a meeting in Newport. Old Dog could work without interference.

Dog found himself laboring with a coldly determined anger that fueled unsuspected energies. That quick, almost overnight, Bat Stailey had produced a confessed killer, willing to take whatever heat the nation's legal systems could deliver. What sort of specimen would take the rap for Bat Stailey?

On the other hand, why not? Serve-anybody defense lawyers might win on an imaginative self-defense plea—about like Larry had dreamed up.

More likely, a comfortable plea bargain would be arranged. The "volunteer" would plead guilty to simple manslaughter, do eighteen months and some community service, perhaps a heavy fine (which Stailey's organization would pay with pocket change) and be free to enjoy whatever rewards the mob had promised. Bat Stailey would never be in the picture again.

Well, almost never. Instead of his attorneys quietly closing out the paperwork involved in his arrest, Stailey would personally appear at the courthouse in Harrisburg. The Teflon Don desired a moment in the sun. He would, as he had before, stand on the courthouse steps and declare his outrage at his false arrest and the police vendetta against him. The press would be there, sucking it up to vomit forth on radio, TV, and in news columns. Old Dog planned on providing a better headline.

From among the guns stacked in closet corners, Old Dog chose a battered but serviceable double-barrel 12-gauge shotgun. The old cannon had been around since he and Larry were young men. They had long owned better guns, and the double had not been fired in years. It would shoot as well as ever, Old Dog was certain. He examined the bores and clicked the triggers. The internal hammers fell fast and solid sounding.

He held the shotgun in their workbench vise while he wrapped electrical tape tightly around the wooden forearm and barrels. Then he hacksawed away all but fourteen inches of the barrels and all but the butt stock behind the grip. The result was a mean looking sawed-off shotgun capable of being easily hidden.

Without barrel choke, whatever shot load was fired would spread rapidly. The sawed-off still had to be pointed right, but whatever it hit got hit all over. Citizens who howled about Uzis, AK 47s, and 9mm pistols in the hands of the lawless should be grateful that the same villains did not prefer shotguns. If they did, the street carnage might double or triple.

The law could not confine Bat Stailey, so Old Dog would eliminate him. He could attempt that where an ordinary citizen could not because death hovered in the wings and would soon take him. He was already beyond punishing. Bat Stailey's demise, would after all, cap Old Dog's newly constructed monument to society.

Of course, that same society would brand him a vigilante murderer. Media outcry would condemn the illegal taking up of arms against the bad guy. Their plea would be for more and better laws, courts, judges—the very things their continual carping, nitpicking, and ridiculing had made grossly ineffectual.

In Old Dog's opinion, the American free press was both blessing and curse. Few would deny its necessity to expose and explain, but the assorted media also inflamed and exacerbated. It exaggerated and distorted. It was usually just a little bit incorrect, and at times it flat-out lied.

To get the story, the media inflated and ignored common sense, courtesy, privacy, security, and consequences. Responsibility, Old Dog believed, was positioned far down the media priority scale.

The news media would be right to savage anyone who shotgunned another. Old Dog found no fault with that. Unfortunately, the same vehement critics were rarely as willing to pile on the bitter adjectives when mentioning the perpetually immoral—the mobsters, the sleazy lawyers, or the political bloodsuckers.

Though they would deny heatedly, when dealing with the big boys, power, position, money, and influence leavened the media's word selections.

Let 'em howl. Old Dog dropped a pair of single-o buckshot shells into the sawed-off double barrel's chambers. He closed the action, appreciating the still solid snick of closely machined steel. The tang safety was automatic. Until he thumbed it forward, the shotgun would not fire.

The Yamaha purchased in Daytona was next. He had stashed the motorcycle in an old shed behind a Marklesville farm. Tim and Larry believed he had given it away. Externally, the cycle was a rolling disaster. Rusted, scraped, and bent here and there, the bike looked like junk, but it ran with a tight-cylindered fury that could pop a wheel on demand.

Old Dog dug out a long ignored full face helmet, dusted off the plastic face piece, and kick started the Yamaha. He cut a few figure eights before broad sliding through a number of over-fast turns on the dirt trace leading across their property.

Dog felt the unaccustomed weakness of arm and leg, but riding a scooter was like walking. As long as balance held out, he could do it.

Yet, even the few minutes of familiarizing tired him badly, and the ache across his lower back pounded unmercifully. He rode the cycle onto the positioned pickup and tied it down. He covered the cycle carefully. He had no doubt it would appear on television, and he did not want some casual observer recalling that Old Dog Carlisle had a machine like that.

Bat Stailey's media event would go off at two PM. That would allow plenty of time for editing before the evening news. Old Dog hoped public attendance would not be large. His plan approached foolhardy and contained too many seeds of disaster. A touch of ill luck could thwart his best effort, but he had no extra time. Old Dog saw no other way.

Stailey's house would now be an unapproachable fortress. Someone had set up Stailey, and the gangster would suspect an inside job. What outsider could have known about the money stash?

The coincidence of trying to stuff his derringer into the bathrobe pocket holding Stailey's money cache still tickled Old Dog's fancy. There had been seven thousand dollars in the packet. A handsome and unexpected bonus, and a valuable byproduct was Bat Stailey's probable belief in inside betrayal. Unfortunately, the mobster would be heavily guarded at home.

On the road, Stailey had his limo. Some said the car was bulletproof. Perhaps it was not, but its tinted windows hid occupants. Without knowing where Stailey sat, Old Dog could not just ride alongside and blast him with the shotgun.

The photo and press opportunity was the best chance. If Old Dog had preparation time, a distant sniping hide might have been found. Or, close study might have proven it practical to shoot from a little way out and ride away. The problem there could be shifting and unanticipated crowd movement. A clear shot might prove impossible. Old Dog did not have practice runs to find out.

There was one sure way, but it was not so certain that he could ride away unscathed, which, to come full circle, was why he and he alone was singularly equipped to do the job.

Unlike his planned execution of Hunch Watson, Old Dog would just go for it and hope for the best.

The vigilante would gallop his bronc into town, gun down the evil gambler, and ride into the sunset (a big maybe there) while grateful town folk gazed admiringly after him. Ha! Any admiring would not happen or be admitted publicly, but if Stailey went down, many a TV watcher would privately echo Old Dog Carlisle's own thoughts of "Got the bastard at last!"

It was still mid-morning, so he had a lot of time. A nap now was sort of essential. Old Dog would take his pain killers and buffer their impact on his sensitive stomach with a milkshake. He would sleep until noon, then motor on down to Harrisburg.

Stailey would not be early lest a news team arrive late. Old Dog would have time for a quick reconnoiter and selection of a waiting sight. When Bat Stailey started talking, Old Dog Carlisle would deliver thirteen or maybe the full twenty-six buckshot packed into his double gun. Dog doubted Stailey could digest all of them.

Chapter 19

Bat Stailey waited inside the courthouse with some impatience. It was not the best of times. The thought of the trap set for him, certainly by someone close, curdled his guts, and he still was not clear of it. The confessed killer could still recant, although such a foolhardy action was improbable. There had, in fact, been serious discussion as to when it would be best to eliminate the man.

One camp believed he should permanently disappear just before trial. The law could then spend eternity looking for him. Another side preferred elimination in prison following conviction. That solution closed the case. Stailey hoped that the confessor would be granted his rewards and the promised safety; he recalled a similar situation when a lawyer had appeared with witnessed and notarized damning statements by an associate too hastily terminated.

Those were only part of Bat Stailey's worry.

Powers far greater than Stailey were edgy. The organization did not like police investigations. Public interest in their activities was unwelcome. Images became tarnished, and who knew what might be uncovered.

Prominent individuals like Bat were expected to wear clean skirts. They were to be likeable, socially acceptable, and handsome—if possible, the kind of men others admired and respected. Hints of mob connections could add a touch of titillation, but nothing dirty should cling.

Stailey had long been an epitome of such a man. His too-close association to a double slaying required immediate public explanation and personal distancing. Bat intended his courthouse appearance—emphasizing unremitting harassment, personal indignation, and unequivocal innocence—to be a powerhouse.

The law had thought they had Bat Stailey cold, and the unexpected confession fell like a bomb amid their expectations. At the moment, the prosecutors and investigators were on the ropes, and Stailey intended hammering so hard they would be extremely leery of trying for him again.

Although he would have preferred having his attorneys handle everything, Stailey's very prominence demanded a public appearance. His familiar craggy features with his majestic crown of thick, gray hair was often featured at social and philanthropic gatherings.

Persons of power, men of respect, were expected to stand tall and to speak out. False accusations and personal affronts could not be tolerated, and Stailey's indignation would be understood and shared.

Everyone despised lawyers, and many citizens had serious doubts about law enforcement's sense of justice. Stailey intended to feed those dislikes and confusions. He expected that following his press interview his social presence would be in increased demand. Many would simply be hoodwinked. Others would desire his presence much as a viewer is attracted to a safely confined serpent. Hints of danger, mystery, and intrigue were irresistible to some. Rumors of CIA, FBI, and Cosa Nostra connections added spice to humdrum lives. Bat Stailey could emerge whistle clean and still be Harrisburg's acceptable bad boy. "The man you just have to have at your next social affair."

It was time. Bat checked his appearance—tie knotted dead center, perfect fitting jacket pulled tightly downward so no material rolled behind the neck, sharply creased trousers. Television stared mercilessly at such usually minor details. Noses must never wrinkle. Lips could not be moistened by an errant tongue, and avoid eyes darting and blinking. Look regal, elegant, above the pettiness forced upon you—that was the ticket.

No bodyguards could be present. Hard guys with suspicious underarm bulges would be contrary to the solid citizen demeanor. Flanked by a pair of lawyers, at least as well known as himself, Bat went forth. The waiting reporters began addressing their microphones, centered above the speaking spot, and cameras were focused on them.

Mixing a greeting smile with eye flashing determination and outrage, Stailey took his place.

Two microphones were on stands, and a reporter sat low on the step holding aloft a third. Hand-held TV cameramen braced their backs against curb parked cars, and a pair of still photographers snapped away. Stailey wondered idly what they did with all the photos. Only one or two would ever appear in print.

Off to the left a motorcycle fired up. Its explosive rap caused a soundman to curse, and Stailey permitted a slight frown of annoyance to touch his brow. Until the noise abated, he would wait.

The cyclist wore a white upper garment and seemed slim. His features were lost behind a plastic face shield. The rider eased his machine into the approaching lane with a careful, unhurried grace. Inwardly Stailey fumed, but he looked away, smiling condescendingly into the cameras, allowing the delay to increase his empathy with the equally annoyed reporters.

Old Dog had cruised into Harrisburg an hour early. No crowd gathered before the courthouse, but they would come. Journalists worked with deadlines. They would arrive just in time, do their work, and be gone as quickly. No fuss, just a job to do.

Dog parked his pickup in an alley south of the square. He chose a spot where he could back against a high, protruding cement curb. That flattened his ramp's angle and made unloading the motorcycle less difficult.

The Yamaha was not a Harley. Hundreds of pounds lighter, it once would have offered no challenge. In his weakened condition, Old Dog had his work cut out, but he got the bike down and the kickstand out. Instantly exhausted and more than a little dizzy, he sat sidesaddle and let his wind come back. Phlegm clogged his breathing, and he hocked and spat it loose. Were there blood specks? He was not sure. God, what a mess he was, and why bother with all this? Nobody gave a hoot in hell about Bat Stailey anyway.

But he did! He had chosen to tackle the job, and he would see it through. One last danger-filled, worthwhile effort—it really was that—so he would do it.

And, it might well be his last effort. His plan was little more than a shop window smash, grab, and run. You relied on confusion and luck to get away. Sometimes it worked, but often it did not. One alert cop standing in the way could end a get away before he rode ten feet. Old Dog felt his heart begin to pump with adrenalin excitement.

Too soon for that. He had to husband what little energy and strength he had, because he was not going to just down Bat Stailey and roll over. He intended to escape, and that could require hard riding and lengthy effort.

Old Dog climbed into the truck cab and dozed away a half hour.

The day was brisk with overcast sky. Wind off the Susquehanna was sharp. It was a gloves and leather jacket day, but Old Dog's motorcycle jacket was rolled in the Harley Davidson's saddlebag, high in their barn peak. Instead, he pulled a white dress shirt over a denim jacket. The shirt afforded no protection, but if he rode free of close pursuit, he could shed the thing and disguise his appearance.

He hated full face helmets, but the plastic mask completely hid his features, and on a chill day like this one it was a welcome shield.

Dog laid the sawed-off shotgun across his thighs and draped an ancient towel over it. The muzzles lay to the right. He would shoot left handed. The Yamaha idled poorly, and his right hand would be busy with the cycle's throttle. He would bring the cycle to a halt in neutral using the foot brake. He would grip the gun, flick off the safety with his thumb, and shoot from beneath his extended right arm. The shotgun would kick like hell, up against his arm he hoped. If it did, he might control the damned cannon enough for a second barrel. Then, drop the gun onto his thighs, get the machine into gear, and ride like the very devil was in hot pursuit. He intended to be gone before shock wore off and people leaped at him or got their own guns working. It sounded routinely simple enough. He wondered if it would be.

Dog rode easily up Second Street, turned left and again left onto Front. He turned left a third time onto the courthouse street. Parking was easy. It usually was for motorcycles. Almost any gap would do. Dog backed the Yamaha into the curb, kickstanded, cut the engine, and relaxed.

Microphones were going up, and a reporter stood as if speaking for camera focusing. No one glanced Old Dog's way. A traffic cop was keeping cars moving. Dog took notice of the officer's quick draw pistol rig. The day of poor-shooting policemen with green, corroded cartridges frozen into ancient .38-caliber revolvers was gone. The streets were mean, and police had learned about pistol practice. How good and how quick a shot this officer was remained to be seen. His back tingling in apprehension, Old Dog wished he owned body armor.

Bat Stailey came out. His appearance was on schedule, but unannounced, and Old Dog felt suddenly unready. He steeled his nerve, and as Stailey took position on the steps, Dog kicked over the Yamaha. The engine caught loud and strong. Stailey glanced over and then disinterestedly away as Old Dog eased into the traffic lane.

As he had expected, the sidewalk between the speaker and the cameras lay empty. Like a classroom, Old Dog thought, everybody crowded the back.

The reporter holding a mike up to Stailey was a worry. Dog wanted no innocent victims. Stailey's lawyers ranged aggressively alongside their client, looking grave and offended. Highly effective, Old Dog believed. They held the cameras' attention, waiting for Dog's engine noise to subside.

His heart thudding, mouth suddenly parched, fearful of wetting his pants, Old Dog began his move into traffic. His lungs ached for air, his muscles felt like Jello. God, he'd never make it!

Then, without warning, with the skill of a thousand repetitions, Dog horsed the cycle over the curb and onto the sidewalk. He powered ahead, causing an observer to leap cursing aside, and he was there. He braked hard, booting into neutral, the Yamaha rocking on its suspension. Bat Stailey looked down at him, perhaps annoyed, but appearing regally above it all.

Doubts and anxieties buried, the cameras, spectators, and policeman forgotten, Old Dog's left hand gripped the sawed-off shotgun. His thumb slid away the safety. His concentration lasered on Bat Stailey's form, Dog snapped the gun up beneath his right arm just as he had planned. Acutely aware of consternation altering Stailey's patrician features, the seated reporter's frantic collapse and the lawyers' belated cringes away were barely peripheral.

Cold—as controlled as he had been those forty or so years past when he had killed other enemies until he went down himself—Old Dog Carlisle fired his first barrel point-blank into Bat Stailey's chest.

Irritation at the unexpected delay rode Bat Stailey. Timing in large part controlled an audience, and here he had to stand attempting to appear dominant, waiting out the racket of some fool on a motorcycle. If he had the power, Stailey would have murdered the idiot

With mounting disbelief he saw the cyclist cut back onto the sidewalk and power his way to a skidding halt directly before him.

Unnoticing, the traffic cop wagged his baton at leisurely moving automobiles. Stailey swore he would have the half-wit's badge.

The cyclist's black plastic mask was turned blankly toward him. Only then did the cold menace in the rider's lean frame strike Bat Stailey.

As if in slow motion, Stailey saw the twin muzzles of a shotgun appear below the rider's right armpit. Within his horror, Stailey's mind asked who had ordered and paid for the hit. Names flashed as he wished his body into motion, knowing he would have someone's soul for this. Until the buckshot struck, Bat Stailey did not consider that he was going to die.

The shotgun bucked like a mule, but Old Dog did not feel it. He saw the microphones in front of Stailey disintegrate, and a large piece struck Stailey's face. The blast ruffled Stailey's coat and shirt, as if a powerful fan had swung past. The big form appeared to deflate a little just before Old Dog squeezed his second trigger.

There seemed to be a lot of smoke, more than there should be, Old Dog thought, but there was no doubt his charges had gone home. The first barrel had frozen Stailey in place. The second shot-load buckled him like a jackknife. Old Dog stomped the Yamaha into gear and fed in power. The rear tire squalled on concrete, caught traction, and the motorcycle burst into motion.

The acceleration slid Old Dog back in his saddle, but he leaned forward, avoiding a wheely, keeping his front wheel on the sidewalk for steering. The shotgun balanced precariously across his lap but stayed on.

Dog held to the sidewalk, driving for distance between his exposed back and possible shooters. The police officer was in the street and would have to gain the sidewalk to make a shot. Dog heaved around an astonished pair of pedestrians, glad to have them between himself and the policeman.

There was no time to consider how he had done. The run was like racing motorcross; he wove around walkers and rocketed across an alley's curbing. He hit the Second Street corner as hard as his machine could go. Dog muscled the Yamaha into a side-slipping right turn, right foot down and sliding, accelerating out, seeking protection behind intervening buildings. Second Street traffic traveled north. Old Dog stayed on the sidewalk and went south. Against the grain, he would be hard to follow.

The unexpected attack and cold-blooded execution stunned and paralyzed. Cameramen filmed automatically, their minds barely comprehending. One managed to follow the fleeing murderer, zooming in closely and holding until the rider disappeared. The others stayed on the chaos on the courthouse steps.

The steps reporter, his microphone still working, babbled wildly, attempting to record his observations and impressions. A lawyer huddled above Stailey's blasted form. The other had fainted and lay unmoving. For minutes, it was believed he too had been shot. The traffic policeman only belatedly realized that something awkward had happened. He did not even see the motorcyclist escape.

Confusion ruled. Men screamed for ambulances, and journalists spoke frantically and sought other views. The lone policeman hollered into his hand-held radio, but for long minutes no pursuit was mounted, and for many more minutes no one had much of a description of the "Killer Biker"—the name quickly adopted by the media.

Old Dog found a traffic gap and slashed across Second Street. He wove around to reach his alley and the parked pickup. He rammed onto his ramp and slammed to a halt in the truck bed, striking the cab end so hard he expected a cycle wheel had bent.

Dog let the Yamaha fall on its side. He dropped to the ground, heaved the ramp into the truck bed, and slammed the tailgate. The alley remained deserted, but who could tell if eyes saw from behind the dozens of overlooking windows?

His breathing rasped like fingernails on a chalkboard. His hands shook, and strength was flowing away. But there was still much to do. Dog scrambled back onto the truck. He flipped his tarp onto the laid-over Yamaha concealing it completely. Still helmeted and wearing the white shirt, Old Dog climbed behind the wheel and drove away.

Alleys connected. He made two turns before again pulling over. Inside the truck he shed shirt and helmet. Ahead a trash dumpster beckoned. Dog pulled alongside, ripped the shirt into strips, and tossed it inside.

Another one hundred feet along a sewer drain yawned at curbside. Dog pulled up and listened to the welcome gurgle of underground water. He broke open the sawed off and extracted the empty shells. A quick flip and slide consigned the incriminating empties and gun to the

Harrisburg sewer system. Only then did Old Dog remove his gloves.

He motored then, mixing in traffic, taking his time out to the Farm Show area. He parked amid student vehicles in the HAAC lot. With a cynical grin, he laid his full face helmet on a nearby bench. If it stayed there long, he would be surprised.

The ache in his back was horrid, and he was too tired to do more. At least he was not coughing up bits of his lungs. Old Dog swallowed a pair of Demerol pills and waited for their effect.

Finally, he could consider how it had gone. Strange, now that it was done, he really did not care about the outcome. If it turned out that Stailey somehow lived, Dog guessed it would no longer matter. Burned out on it, he supposed.

No one else had gotten hurt. He could be reasonably sure of that blessing. Someone could have shot wildly, but he had not detected firing. Dog tried to remember sound, but it was strangely absent, as though a mute button had been pressed. He recalled strained faces and awkward movements. The strike of buckshot into Stailey was clear in his mind's vision. He could feel the motorcycle's heaving violence as he fled, but until he turned onto Second Street, there was no sound. Odd, but in a way comforting. He did not need the shotgun's blasts or shouts and screams to confuse memories.

Of course, he had not felt the lightened shotgun's heavy recoil. On targets, a shotgunner suffered recoil, but in the field the same kick went unremarked. The heavy smoke? Perhaps from shortened barrels. It was odd that in such a tension-packed moment he would have noticed.

The Demerol took hold, dulling nerve endings and relaxing overstressed systems. Old Dog guessed he would live after all ... but just for a little while longer, he was sure.

He had gotten away more cleanly than he could have hoped. After resting, he would clean the oiled muck off his truck's license plate. He supposed no one had seen the bike's unloading or reloading, but if they had, getting the truck's license number would have taken careful and close examination.

A nagging fear had been that someone would have stolen his cycle ramp while he was gone. If he had returned to find himself rampless, he had planned on dousing the Yamaha with gasoline, lighting it, and driving away. Nowhere near as good. Now, all he had left to do was drive up to Bloomfield and dump the Yamaha into Fred Thebes's deep hole. He would kick in enough shale to hide the bike. Soon Fred would fill the hole with tailings, and the machine would be buried forever.

First he would rest. Another hour should do. At home, his VCR was faithfully recording Channel 21. No doubt the cable was already burning with coverage of the dastardly crime.

Screw 'em. Bat Stailey was history, and Old Dog Carlisle was pleased to have done it.

Chapter 20

Just after dark, rain had begun to fall. The temperature dropped with it, and weatherman Chuck Rhodes spoke about various fronts milling about

Old Dog had gotten in before that. He had hoofed in sock-footed, his second pair of jump boots buried with the Yamaha. His gloves were there as well, and he would like to have thrown in his pants, but arriving bare-butted would have been noticed. The pants would go out in the next trash pickup. The TV cameras had surely recorded close details, but his pants should be the last identifiable item.

Larry and Timmy had come over after supper to watch the evening news, which would carry the first complete coverage of the Bat Stailey assassination.

Timmy had ideas. "It was probably a biker friend of the one that Stailey killed in his woods. Bikers get even, Dad."

"More likely his own mob rubbed him out."

"In front of TV cameras, Larry?" Old Dog sounded doubtful. "Stailey was big. If the bosses wanted him dead they would have had him disappear Jimmy Hoffa style."

Larry said, "The killer was a young whippy guy. He tossed that motorcycle around like it was a toy."

"Uncle Dog used to ride like that. Didn't you, Uncle Dog?"

"Used to is right, Tim. My biking days are past."

"You could still ride, Uncle Dog."

"Maybe, but it would be mighty gentle highway cruising." Old Dog chuckled. "If the bike fell over it would have to lay there. I'd never get it up again."

He chuckled again. "Maybe I'll get a Gold Wing."

"Oh, Uncle Dog, you wouldn't ride one of those things. They ought to have four wheels. They aren't hardly real motorcycles."

Larry was wry, "You taught him well, Adam."

The Stailey coverage was stunning. The local stations had pooled their film. What one had missed, another had managed.

For Old Dog, the watching was disconcerting. The masked biker did appear young, lean, and wire muscled. Had that been him? Of course, but ... God, he looked good. Unbelievable!

Old Dog watched the rest with detachment. If there had been censoring, it had been minimal.

As he remembered, a microphone had slammed into Stailey's face, and the mobster's shirt had rippled as buckshot pellets—some distorted from striking microphones—drove into his chest

The second blast followed so closely its report blended with the first. Stailey doubled and fell forward, down the steps to sprawl face hidden on the concrete.

Whew, it was graphic! The perfectly focused action was caught in such detail it appeared movie-like, as though actors had staged it all. Even the killer's escape zoomed in tight

Larry said, "No license plate on the bike."

"It's an old Rice Burner." Tim's voice was disdainful. To Timmy and many Harley riders, other makes were beneath identification. "They all looked alike."

The rider's broadsliding turn onto Second Street was handsome. Old Dog wondered how he had managed it.

Timmy was admiring. "That's a motocross rider, Uncle Dog. I can tell 'em every time."

"Probably right, Tim. Man can really ride."

Larry reminded, "Let's not get admiring. The rider is a cold-blooded killer, remember, almost certainly a paid hitman."

"Think they'll get him, Dad?"

"Sooner or later, probably. Those kinds of people have friends, too. They talk, then someone gets mad, and word leaks out." Larry was certain of one thing. "With the coverage this shooting is getting, the law won't dare back off. They'll all be hunting."

"Maybe it'll be somebody you know, Uncle Dog. You know a lot of bikers."

"Not many young ones, Tim. Most of my friends are old guys."

Because he was obviously feeling lousy, Larry and Tim left early. Old Dog showered and eased gratefully into bed. Dosed with painkiller, he had only minutes to consider what he had seen. Hair showed beneath the masked rider's helmet. He would get a shorter haircut. Otherwise, Dog saw nothing traceable—except his pants, and they would be gone tomorrow.

He experienced no inner glow of satisfaction, and that disappointed him. What were his feelings? Just glad to have it done with, he decided.

So, it really was finished. He could forget Bat Stailey, Clout, and Hunch. His personal gift to the world was as complete as he would make it.

Had he accomplished anything real or lasting? Probably not. Few individuals genuinely altered the course of human events, but perhaps he had dented the historical record just a trifle.

Good or bad, important or insignificant, he, Old Dog, had made his move and had seen it through. That was about all anyone ever accomplished in life. Perhaps he was satisfied after all.

As if answering a summons, a pair of easyriders appeared early at Old Dog's door. Old acquaintances, they had heard Dog was not going to make it. They had ridden up from York to wish him the best and to say goodbye.

Before they left, another rode in. He came from Lancaster. The rider could not recall how the news was passing, he had just heard it.

Old Dog knew. That damned Stool had let it out. It had to be Stool. No other brothers knew. Correction: No other brothers had known. Dog heard more Harley engines moving along Main Street.

Well, it was Saturday and bikers hunted reasons to ride on their weekends. It was nice of them to come. Old Dog decided he was not mad at Stool after all. Maybe all the dope he was taking had mellowed him.

And they kept coming, single riders, some with their camps behind their saddles. Many riding double, their latest women all leathered out and strutting proud.

Arlis fled inside and finally left for Harrisburg, Larry in tow. Timmy stayed, glorying in every arrival. He and a biker he had met in Daytona took Old Dog's pickup to Newport on a beer run. Dog sat on his porch greeting vistors and marveling that so many friends, acquaintances, and even strangers bothered.

Sunday was no better, and Arlis complained that her weekend was ruined, and that she couldn't wait until Monday when everyone would get back to work. Only, on Monday they kept riding in. Some bikers, Arlis had forgotten, did not work all that regularly.

Old Dog wore out easily. He would sack out, only to find riders waiting for his waking. Often he dozed in his rocker, heavily sedated, wrapped in his old blanket, while brothers reminisced and drank his or their own beer. Some camped for a night behind the barn. Others only shook hands and rode on. Old Dog felt like an expiring prelate whose loyal subjects passed for a final touch of hand or eye. An old rider brought his son to meet the suddenly legendary Old Dog Carlisle. An entire club came down from Tioga County—fourteen Harley riders Dog had never known existed.

Timmy found a grizzled biker sitting on a hay bale in their barn weeping into his beard. "They just don't make 'em like Old Dog anymore."

It was Stool all right, and on Thursday Stool himself came trundling in riding a trike built out of an old knucklehead Harley.

Dog was awake and alert when Stool pulled up and shut down in front of the porch.

Old Dog examined him archly. "What in hell are you riding? Can't you balance anymore?"

Undismayed, Stool came up to shake hands. "As Pythagoras noted, 'Three wheels determine a plane.'" Stool made himself comfortable.

Dog said, "It's you sending these riders in here, isn't it?"

"I don't send them, Dog. I let them know, and they choose to come." Stool smiled, "Sort of astounding though, isn't it?"

Old Dog groused, "Doubt my sister-in-law would choose that description. Another day or two of this, and she'll likely burn me out."

"I'll talk to her." Stool changed the subject.

"*Easyriders* magazine got here yet?"

"What?"

"Well, they're sending someone to interview you."

Old Dog exclaimed, "Holy hell!"

Stool appeared quizzical. "You don't realize it even now, do you, Dog?" He sighed as though having to explain to a child.

"You are one of the big guys, Adam. You've been easyriding before the name was invented, and you are known all over the country. When you pass, people say, 'There goes Old Dog.' You are famous, Dog. Riders like you; they want to be like you. You are a charter member of this way of ours, Adam. Biking is our 'Cosa Nostra, our thing.' It's what we do. It's a society, a club, a brotherhood. Biking is a world within a world, and it's our world.

"The fact is, Dog, we've got leaders—unannounced ones like yourself. We have magazines, social orders, businesses, and hobbies built around biking. If you added it all up, we're more than a billion dollar a year industry."

Old Dog snorted in disgust. "Hell, Stool, we're just guys who like to ride motorcycles. A few of us did it full-time. So what? Most citizens hate our guts. They think we're noisy, dangerous, and dirty. They'd take us off the roads if they could." Dog considered, "In fact, they'll probably do just that somewhere down the line. I'm glad I won't be around to see it."

"That's why we need a written history, Adam. We need our story written down with names and places. The machines need describing, the easyriders, the clubs, the racers, the moms and pops. People need to know how many of us there are—more than belong to the NRA, or NOW, or . . ."

"Ah hah!" Old Dog pointed a bony finger at his friend, who began to smile shyly.

"That's it. That's why you're riding that three wheeler. You've got to pack records around. You're starting to write that history."

Old Dog rocked back in awe. "Man, Stool, that's a big order—to do it right, I mean."

Stool was appropriately humble, "It's big all right, but Adam, I've got it all here in my head and more on paper and in photos in my boxes. I can do it. Three years, I figure, that's what it'll take."

Old Dog was cynical. "Then, who'll publish it, Stool? It'll be a huge thing. What, one thousand photographs, maybe a lot more? How many pages? Fifteen hundred?"

Stool was defensive. "If I can get five hundred copies printed, it'll be enough, Dog. Getting it down so it won't be lost is the thing."

"It'll cost a fortune."

"I've been putting money away for it, Dog."

"How much've you got, Stool? Honest now."

"Damned near ten thousand dollars."

"Ten grand? Geez, Stool, that might get some printed, but what are you going to eat on while you are writing? You'll have to make the rallies or you'll miss new history. For three years, man? You'd better find a woman who'll take care of you."

"I've got a place up in Piercy, California. You remember it, Dog?"

Old Dog

"You mean that old tourist cabin place along the river . . . what was its name?"

"Resting Oak."

"Yeah, hey, that's nice up there, Stool. Gee, those were good times." Dog sighed, "No helmet laws back then." He remembered, "Didn't you grow some pot up on the hill across the river?"

Stool grinned in happy memory. "I was younger then, Dog."

"Yeah, you'd just started riding free."

"I had to eat."

"You planning on growing weed again? You'll have to eat this time, too."

"God, no! That was then. This is now. I'll work it out . . . somehow."

Timmy came from school and took Stool to meet his mother. Old Dog called after them, "I'm going to sleep a while. If I hear gunshots, I'll know Arlis got you."

Arlis liked Adam's friend. He knew a thousand interesting things. Stool, what a peculiar nickname, but many of Old Dog's friends had strange names.

Stool knew wonderful cooking recipes. He appreciated flowers, and he understood exactly Arlis's brand of personal Christianity.

A very nice man, Arlis thought. It was too bad he could not escape the rowdy motorcycling.

Stool stayed at the house for a while, and that gave Old Dog time to consider one last problem and to work out a practical solution.

When Stool came back, Old Dog was rocking on the porch, his head fuzzy with narcotic, but not hurting too bad.

Dog did not beat about the bush. "Stool, I've got a story to tell and a proposition to make. To get the deal I'm offering you've got to agree to real secrecy and a long follow through on what I'm asking."

"What in hell are you talking about, Dog?"

"Here's the proposition. You need money to hold you over while you're writing your masterpiece. Well, it happens I've got money I won't be needing. I'm willing to put it up, if you agree to some requirements."

"What requirements?"

"Nope, it won't work like that. Here's how it is. I'll give you cash money, thirty thousand dollars, for your living and printing expenses, and I'll hand over seven thousand more bucks as payment for your doing what it is I'm asking be done. But you don't get anything until you agree to do what I ask."

"My God, Dog, where did you get money like that?"

"I invested wisely." Hunch's saddlebag delivered the thirty grand and Stailey's pocket produced the other seven thousand smackers—for a good cause, Old Dog figured.

"What do I have to agree to?"

"Damn it, Stool! Are you dumb or something? I told you, you have to agree first. Then I'll tell you."

"Strange way to deal. It must be something awful."

"Try trusting me, Stool."

"Try trusting me, Dog."

"I will, as soon as you agree."

Dog held up a restraining hand. "We'll talk about it later, here comes Timmy."

A car also pulled into the yard. Two men in suits got out. They appeared uncertain for a moment, glancing toward the house, then at Dog's shanty with Stool's parked trike and people on the porch. They started back, looking serious and business-like.

"You know 'em, Tim?"

"I don't, Uncle Dog. They look like insurance men to me, though. Probably hunting Dad."

The pair came close and halted.

"Adam Carlisle? Official sounding, Dog thought.

"That's me."

"I'm Special Agent Maxwell, and this is Agent Calder, Federal Bureau of Investigation. We would like a few words with you."

Dog turned to Stool in apparent amazement. "Holy hell, Stool, FBI. Hard to believe."

He turned back to the agents. "Come on up. Find seats. This is Stool, and that's my nephew, Tim."

The agents shook hands, and Old Dog said, "Aren't you supposed to show ID or something? Or is this an unofficial visit?"

Maxwell offered his identification. It was unusual for an agent to more than show his papers. Hmmmm! Dog examined the credentials and passed them to an awed Timmy, who studied the plastic closely before handing off to Stool.

"What do you want to talk to me about?" Old Dog's voice was barely curious. At Maxwell's questioning glance, he added, "Stool and Tim will sit in, if it's all right."

"We are investigating the murder of Mister Batey Stailey. I expect you have heard about it"

"Hell, yes, I've heard about it. I'm glad somebody finally got that bastard. Four of his hired thugs beat hell out of me a few years back."

"You knew, Mister Stailey?"

"No, but we all knew about him. The law should have put him away years ago."

"Did you happen to know Mister Joseph Watson?"

"I don't recall the name." Old Dog did not wish to appear too knowledgeable.

"You know a Joseph Watson, Stool?" Dog asked.

"That was Hunch's real name, Dog." Stool sounded a bit ironic, Dog thought.

"Oh, Hunch. Yeah, I knew Hunch. A sorry, lousy, good-for-nothing to my thinking. I figure Stailey killed him, even if another guy did confess."

"And Mister Clout, did you know him as well?"

"Nope. I was never introduced to him." A small evasion there.

"We understand that you have a permit to carry a concealed weapon."

"Yep, had one since back in the fifties."

"We heard you sometimes carry a five-shot derringer type pistol."

"Now how did you know that?"

Calder, apparently the junior agent, appeared smug, but Maxwell was all business.

"A motorcyclist shot Mister Stailey, and Mister Watson, a cyclist, was killed along with Mister Clout, involving Mister Stailey. Our investigations have included both motorcycle and firearms directions. Your name surfaced in each investigation."

"Now that is amazing." Old Dog was genuinely astonished. The linkage had seemed remote, but he was prepared.

"We would like to see your pistol, Mister Carlisle."

Old Dog nodded. "I follow you. You figure I might have shot Clout and left my gun to incriminate Stailey."

Dog snorted disdainfully. "I guess you know there are thousands of those pistols out there, don't you?"

"We try to check everything, Mister Carlisle." Maxwell was firm.

"Tim, you know where I keep the pistol. Bring it here. Remember, it's loaded." Agent Calder unobtrusively unbuttoned his suit coat and slid a hand inside. Careful man, Old Dog thought, and not unwise. A loaded weapon was about to appear, and in this day and age anything could happen.

Dog said, "Have you taken a good look at me?"

Agent Maxwell did the answering. "Yes, we have."

"Then you will notice that I'm sick. Damned sick in fact." He held out a skeletal hand. "I'm dying of cancer. My skin is yellowing from liver failure, I haven't swallowed anything but milkshakes and pills in a month, and I've got just about enough strength left to get to the john. In a week or two I will be dead.

"Do you really think I'm the guy you're looking for?"

Agent Maxwell remained unapologetic. "Probably not, Mister Carlisle, but we try to check everything. We still wish to see your pistol."

Timmy reappeared and handed the derringer to Old Dog. Dog accepted the gun gingerly, holding it between two fingers. "Huh, doubt if it's been fired, although I picked it up used. Still holds the cartridges that came with it." Dog handed the pistol to Stool, who glanced at it casually before relaying to Agent Maxwell. Calder's hand was again in view.

Agent Maxwell examined the tiny pistol and jotted its serial number on a pad.

Old Dog said, "If I wasn't about to leave this planet, I'd object real loud to you taking down the number of my gun. We don't have gun registration yet, and unless my weapon is involved in a crime, you shouldn't have its number."

Maxwell's jaw muscles bunched a little, but his voice remained calm. "If your pistol is not involved, its serial number will not go beyond this file."

Old Dog was adamant. "You don't get it, do you? The point is, you don't have a right to it at all if it is not a crime gun. You have the pistol that killed Clout, so mine isn't it. So, why record my number?"

Maxwell replaced his notebook and stood. Agent Calder followed his example. He had wished to ask more, but Carlisle was clearly turning hostile. Jotting down the pistol's number had been a mistake. Carlisle was right. As far as they knew, the gun did not figure in the case. Country people could be damned touchy about their rights to be left alone.

The agent saw no further progress in this interview. They could return if necessary, but judging Carlisle's appearance, it would have to be soon.

Maxwell said, "I'm sorry you feel that way, Mister Carlisle." He placed the pistol on Old Dog's side stand. "We may have to return but probably not."

Maxwell extended a hand, and Old Dog accepted, still appearing miffed. Calder nodded, and the agents departed.

Stool watched the FBI drive away.

"You roweled them pretty good, Dog. Closed their interview right down."

Stool did not miss much, Old Dog recognized. Dog said, "Tim, take off for a while. Stool and I've got some serious palaver to work at."

"I've got to take my workout anyway, Uncle Dog. I'll be out in the barn pumping iron."

Dog said, "Now, where were we?"

"You were about to tell me something secret."

"After you cross your heart and hope to die that you'll keep what I say one hundred percent confidential, and then do what I ask."

Stool sighed, "All right, Old Dog, I give in. I accept the bribe and promise to do whatever it is you want . . . short of maiming or killing, that is."

Old Dog got grim. "It's a deal." He insisted on a binding handshake.

"Here it is then. I killed both Hunch and Clout."

Stool never blinked. "I had that figured."

"You did? How . . ."

"First of all, you asked a whole bunch of questions about Hunch down in Daytona. Too many coincidences, Adam. Clout beat you up, you wanted Hunch taken down, same kind of pistol, but I couldn't be sure until you showed the gun. "Stool pointed at the North American Arms Corporation pistol on Dog's stand. That pistol is number D 33345. Your gun, that you showed me one time, was D

34922." Stool chuckled, "Now I haven't checked, but I'll bet the pistol that punched Clout full of holes is serial numbered D 34922. Of course, no one could ever prove that it had been your gun."

"That was my gun's serial number? Holy hell, Stool, I didn't even recall that pistol's number. You're amazing."

"True, though sometimes I wish I could forget more. Too much clutter in my head. Trouble is, I don't know what to forget. Your gun number, for instance, I liked knowing that right now."

"All right, you figured out Hunch and Clout. I also shotgunned Bat Stailey. That was me you saw on TV."

Stool was again nodding. "I didn't guess that, Dog." Stool grinned, "You are a tough old buzzard. You rode that Yamaha like a kid would." Stool's eyes squinted. "I heard you bought a Jap bike down in Daytona." Stool appeared chagrined, "I should have made the connection."

"I'm sure glad you're on my side, Stool." Old Dog meant it.

It was unburdening to tell someone. Old Dog took his time explaining his wish to end meaningful—doing something worthwhile that no one else could be expected to manage.

Stool seemed to understand. He nodded often and became caught up in Old Dog's descriptions of how he had done it all, and finally, how he felt about it.

Before he was done, Timmy had finished weightlifting and had gone to his house.

Old Dog said, "Now we've come to your part, Stool.

"It's possible that down the road some innocent guy might get blamed for what I did. The guy who confessed to save Stailey has already recanted and is out. Hell, I doubt they'll even charge him with perjury or false confessing or anything else.

"Anyway, I don't want some innocent person suffering, so," Old Dog removed a small paper-wrapped package from the side stand drawer. "This is a typed explanation and description about like I just told to you. I tried to cover everything, like where I got the wire and, of course, where the Yamaha is buried. That should be the clincher. I also wrote out a confession, so my signature would be there, and I inked my right thumb print over part of my mark. My fingerprints are on file from my military days.

"Your job will be to subscribe to the Harrisburg Patriot and the York newspaper, whatever its name is, for the next ten years. You'll check them to make sure no one gets nailed because of me. That isn't at all likely. I figure Stailey will be blamed, but who can tell?

"OK, that isn't all. After ten years, when Tim is old enough to handle it and maybe understand, you're to mail the confession anonymously to the FBI. That will close the case once and for all. Hell, with a little luck, the closing won't get big press coverage and the Carlisles will never know."

Stool nodded affirmation all the way through, but he waited a bit before commenting.

"All right, Dog. I'll do it with one suggestion. Let's make it fifteen years before I send in the confession. A man of thirty, about what Tim will be—won't he?—can handle things a heap better than he would at twenty-five."

"Well, that might be better, Stool, but you'll be as old as the hills by then. Hell, you'll be pushing seventy."

"I'm only fifty, Adam. If some grandma doesn't plow me under with her Pontiac, I'll be around."

"That's what I thought, and look at me."

"You didn't live right."

"Didn't live right? Hell, Stool, I didn't smoke or drink, and I . . ."

"The trouble with you, Dog, is that . . ."

Chapter 21

It was no longer pain. It had become gut grinding agony that nothing suppressed for long. Old Dog sweat and he vomited convulsively and too often—dry heaved from a stomach no longer able to digest solids. Hours of alertness became less than those of drug-induced sleep or stupor. Will and caring faltered.

Old Dog could not doubt that it was time. The great question was—had he waited too long? His was not a simple scheme of walking to a local lookout and swilling narcotic until his systems surrendered.

He had wished for a final adventure, a great all-consuming terminal challenge. He had publicly discussed it for a decade. He had privately weighed and firmed details for even longer. Now it was here, and what had sounded difficult but practical began to feel impossible and foolish—as he had expected it would.

Despite searing gut aches and the lance-like pains that spasmed his chest and lungs, Old Dog began his long planned moves.

His lucid, vigorous enough moments were limited and only generally predictable, so when he could, Dog strove for speed and efficiency.

Old Dog's directions to his chosen travel agent were terse, direct, and as clear as words could be made.

"I am going to Alaska.

"Two days from now, I wish to be picked up by limousine at my front porch in time to meet the most direct flight from Harrisburg to Anchorage that is available.

"At the airport, I must be wheelchair seated and boarded. My tickets must be in first class accommodations.

"On landing at Anchorage, a direct flight to Valdez must be waiting. If no flight is scheduled, a twin engine aircraft must be chartered and waiting. There must be no delay.

"At Valdez a helicopter must be waiting my arrival. It will fly me to milepost 62 on the Richardson Highway. There it will land and leave me. In case of inclement weather, an automobile will be substituted for the helicopter.

"Are there any questions?

"If you fail to confirm everything by this time tomorrow, I will cancel and book with someone else.

"Your limo driver will be paid in full, in cash, upon my arrival at Harrisburg International. Have your bill ready."

Next were the goodbyes.

Larry's took time because there were financial details to settle.

"This shack is now yours, Larry. All else that I have goes to Timmy, but handled as you feel best. It's all included here." Old Dog passed a manila envelope.

"There is also a bequest for you and Arlis. Nothing big, but it will give you a few trips abroad, if you'd like them." Dog grinned through his unremitting pain. "Arlis would like that. It will give her something to make her friends envious."

Dog bid them goodbye together. He had requested no tears, but both Tim and Arlis failed. Larry did little better. Old Dog hurt too much to join in. His concentration had moved on. It was clear he was not coming back, and they were already entering his past.

Old Dog traveled light. He carried no luggage, but beneath a heavy coat he wore his "vest of many pockets." Years before, Arlis had pocketed the old hunting vest. It held the only essentials that his journey demanded. A pocket held a six ounce bottle of seltzer water. Another contained a half pint of whiskey. He had a bottle of Mylanta and the larger bottle of Doctor Philip Klein's powerhouse drug mixture, plus codeine, aspirin, and Demerol. Cripes, he was a walking—well, wheel-chairing—pharmacy, but he could need it all.

A plane change was necessary in Chicago, but he was wheeled about like other baggage. Again airborne for the long hop, Old Dog indulged himself with a stiff swig of Klein's magic and drifted into unconsciousness, remembering kindly the rotund doctor, friend since their youth in Korea. More than forty years. It had been good . . .

The light plane to Valdez made heavy weather of it, but got down safely. The pilot had radioed ahead, and the helicopter waited, blades slowly turning.

Old Dog walked the short distance between aircraft, but required a boost to gain his seat in the chopper, and the minimal effort robbed him of breath. He passed two letters to the fixed wing pilot. "Drop those in the mail for me, will you?"

The pilot would and backed away with an informal salute.

The four-passenger helicopter rose and leaned forward. It darted away like an insect and within moments followed the highway north. To his right rear, Old Dog could see the Valdez pipeline terminus with a tanker loading. But the manmade things of this world no longer held much interest.

He told the pilot, "Follow the road about five hundred feet up. I'll recognize the spot"

The pilot was concerned, "You don't look good, sir. You sure you're all right?"

Old Dog tried not to sound impatient. "No, I'm not all right. In fact, I'm dying, but I know where I want to go. You get me there, and I'll be grateful."

The land climbed and the helicopter with it, but the flight was short. A sixty-two mile road can be much shorter by air. Old Dog easily spotted the cabins.

"OK, see the cabins, two of them off to the right?"

"Sure, I know those. You own 'em?"

"No, I read about them in a novel a few years back. Came up, saw the place, and liked it. Real special back up at the creek head."

Talking tired him, but this would be the last of it. "Set me down on that gravel bar, close to the stream."

"There's no one at those cabins, sir. You sure you want to get out here?"

Dog did not feel up to discussing. "Just set her down and let me out. That's the deal we've got."

"Yes, sir. Going down." To hell with it. If the old goat wanted out, that's what he would get.

Touchdown was nice. Old Dog got his door open. He handed across a folded one hundred dollar bill. "Thanks, pilot, and don't worry about me. It's all planned out."

The pilot watched the staggery old guy get out from under the blades and without a backward glance head for the creek edge. He turned his machine into the wind and added power and collective. Fresh out of the mountains, Ernestine Creek spread wide into a dozen shallow channels. He saw his passenger already crossing, but not heading directly for the cabins.

The pilot made a pass, but the figure had disappeared into the thick spruce and willow thicket along the stream. Maybe the old duffer wasn't as decrepit as he appeared. What the hell, he'd done his part, and a hundred buck tip was all right even by high priced Alaskan standards.

Old Dog lay just within the thicket. It was as far as he could get right now. At least he had gotten hidden. If he had gone down in the open the pilot might have had second thoughts about leaving him.

So far, so good, but he was terribly weak, and that scared him more than the unremitting grind in his guts and lungs and back, and for the first time, a really mean pain in his groin.

He lived now on whatever stores his body had left. There were no Dairy Queens on Ernestine Creek. There was nothing for miles in any direction. Cars might pass on the two lane highway, but even their sound was lost before it could reach him. This was the way he had planned it, but he had not then felt the agonies. Hell, he could die right here beside the stream. What difference would a few hundred yards make?

All the difference! It was always easiest to surrender. Like every human, he had quit more than once when he should have plugged ahead, but this was the last one. He owed it to himself, to all the listeners he had told confidently how he would do it. If they ever needed to find him, he had to be where he had said he would be.

Old Dog got up. The land began a gentle upward slope, and that was his direction. He gripped willows for support and rested every four steps. God, his lungs hurt, but the inhalers no longer helped. Another hour, if he could keep going. Surely he could make that. He took another four steps, then managed another three.

He woke to horrendous groin pain. A scream started in his throat, but he choked it down and rolled over. He had fallen face down, and his pelvis had lain across a mossy rock. No wonder he hurt. Moving helped. In desperation, Old Dog swallowed a not too large dose of Klein's mixture. Not too much he hoped. He was wet to the knees from crossing the stream, and to lie here through an Alaskan night was probably to die here.

How far had he come? A good way apparently. That meant at least two hundred yards in his condition. The hill sloped sharply upward from here. If he could go another two hundred or so, he would be there, but it was steeper than he remembered. So what, he would crawl like an animal. He was not done yet.

First, his marks. He had promised tape to show direction. Old Dog dragged a small roll of blue tape from a vest pocket and made a few waist-high wraps around a tree trunk.

He tried to walk uphill, but his balance really had gotten bad. He slid the tape roll over a finger and crawled on all fours for a few lengths. There he made a second tape wrapping. So it went, crawl a little, wrap tape, with his blood more narcotic than plasma. Five wraps, enough to determine where he had gone. Hunters would come across this slope, and they might wonder at the tapings. Anyone not knowing would assume some peculiar survey or boundary marking and forget it. Old Dog hung his tape roll on a twig and struggled on.

The helicopter had dropped him near midday he supposed. The sun had moved a long way before he broke from the trees. His estimate of an hour had been wide of the mark, but he had rested a lot.

Ahead, not too far either, he saw just what he wanted. An upheaval had raised a stone into a natural backrest, and disturbed earth in front of the stone offered a comfortable seat. Old Dog worked his painful way toward it.

Out of the timber, a crisp breeze dried the dank sweat physical effort or perhaps pain had induced. Old Dog felt a little better and twisted into his high country overlook with a sense of relieved accomplishment.

He had made it. By all the holies, he had. Bright sun had warmed the stone, and its heat on his back was comforting. Old Dog let his breathing slow and looked across what he intended to be his last view of native earth.

The sight was truly magnificent. Craggy peaks rose and fell in splendid disorder. Far below, the creek shown in the sun, shifting from liquid silver to a river of gold as cotton clouds drifted across. Aspen and willow quaked in fresh spring foliage, punctuated by the thrust of taller spruce and trees Old Dog could not name.

He saw a cow moose in a distant creek meadow, the huge creature as natural to the scene as the banked snowfields filling every shadowed hollow. Small wildflowers grew among the green of lichened mountain meadows, and Old Dog felt his pants wetting through from the damp of the not really dry earth he sat on. The ground was still frozen only inches below the surface. This early in the season, snow had barely left the exposed slopes, but Alaskan spring could come in a rush, and it had this year.

A huge crow (was it a raven?) landed nearby and stared at him with fierce eyes. Interesting, he thought In Pennsylvania, a crow's eyes were wary. These birds could be brave. They had not faced man's guns and poisons.

A vicious spasm wracked his chest. Sweat popped on his lips, and his vision blurred. The worst finally passed, but enough pain remained to destroy the pleasure of nature observation.

Old Dog heard himself sigh. He was here, and it was time to get on with what he had come to do.

Freedom from all the gut-rotting, brain-deadening pain. How grand it would be. He smiled grimly inside. Anyone who believed he had chosen the easy way should think again. No hospital would allow the physical agonies he had sweat through, but in the end, he would have the better of it because it would all stop for him. No hoses, no pitying faces, no more pain . . . no more anything.

It would be ludicrous to botch the job at this stage. Old Dog chose to be methodical and deliberate.

He arranged his bottles carefully. First, a healthy slug of Mylanta to settle his stomach (what there was left of it). Then, a few moments relaxation to let the antacid work.

His thoughts wandered. Did God wait for him just beyond awareness? He wished mightily that it could be so. Most of the people he had cared about were already there. Would there really be a heaven with old friends waiting? He had never been able to believe it, but maybe, maybe . . . how marvelous that would be.

Old Dog swallowed seltzer water. Nothing had tasted right for a month, and the bubbly effervescence was no exception. The drink was not for pleasure. Seltzer speeded the action of the important stuff he would take and alcohol would almost double the effectiveness of his drugs. To an abstainer, the impact of booze would undoubtedly be dramatic. He hoped so.

It was important to consume his lethal drugs rapidly. Pill takers sometimes fell asleep before they managed to gulp sufficient numbers and woke up damaged and unsuccessful. Doc Klein's awesomely potent elixir made that error improbable.

Old Dog seized a bottle in each hand. Whiskey in one, Klein's drug mix in the other. He sipped at the alcohol. Vile! He would use the drugs to soften the whiskey's burn. That surely was a switch.

He began the sequence. Whiskey burned his gut like liquid fire—took his breath away. Drugs, a large swallow, all his sensitive throat could manage. Then a gentle pull at the bubbly water.

It was going well. It would work. Old Dog sought anything overlooked. Loosen and open his clothing, that was one. He interrupted his rhythm to unbutton coat, vest, and shirt. If he somehow lingered, the cold night air would finish him. Dog worked at his drinking. He studied the drug bottle. It was way down, but he continued until there was no more. "Thank you, Doc." Old Dog placed the empty aside.

The half pint was also well down, but he feared to attempt finishing the whiskey. It would not do to puke everything up. He had read about that happening. Sitting propped up helped prevent that disaster.

Now he could think the good thoughts he had planned on, and he surely had them. Life had been rich in pleasure and friendships. Bat Stailey touched the fringe of awareness, but Old Dog passed on. Surprisingly, a recent incident began filling his mind. It was a nice one to consider.

He had shared his collected photographs with Stool, photos he had not examined in years. Glancing through he saw himself change from the boy to the warrior to the youthful easyrider with long hair and reckless eyes. Stool might use a few of the photos in his book. The rest would be Timmy's to keep.

One picture, a glossy 8 x 10, stood out. Stool howled in delight, and Old Dog's sick lungs tolerated hoarse laughter at a memory so clearly recorded.

Larry asked, "What in heck is it, Adam?"

"I don't know if I should show it to you, brother. You might feel like your life had been wasted."

"I doubt it."

Old Dog handed the photo to Timmy. "You decide if your Dad should see this, Tim."

The boy looked, and his face flamed. He said, "Wow, Uncle Dog."

"Those were the 1960s, Tim. They could be wonderful times."

Larry demanded, "Let me see that, Tim."

The father studied the photo. His smile broadening, "Well, that is some picture, Adam. It's plain you were enjoying yourself."

Stool said, "It'll be in the book, Old Dog. That's easyriding at its best."

Old Dog again took the photo. "Send Tim a copy, Stool. This would be a good way to remember his uncle Dog instead of the half-alive skeleton he's looking at."

The photograph really was something. Old Dog wished he could remember who had snapped it.

There he was, less than thirty years old. He was astride an old panhead 74-cubic-inch Harley. He remembered the bike well. The photo was a side view. His hair blew back in the wind, and there were giant redwoods beyond the road he traveled.

He rode buck naked, wearing only his jump boots. But, he was not alone. Seated on the gas tank facing him, her head thrown back in laughter, was an equally naked girl of striking proportions. Her golden hair blowing straight in the wind obscured her bright features, and behind him, tight to his back on the old style buddy seat, perched another naked lady. She, too, laughed at the camera with all the tanned, taut-skinned, shining happiness of carefree youth.

It was an exciting photograph. A record of young freedom, long gone, perhaps barely remembered. How sweet it had all been.

Old Dog felt the pain easing throughout his system. His hands and feet enjoyed a curious numbness, as if they were going to sleep.

He looked across the magnificence of the arctic wilderness, but his mind swung again to the glorious day when he had ridden free with the beautiful girls aboard.

He could feel the wind whipping his hair, and the warm California air caressing his tanned nakedness. The road was dry, smooth, and winding enough to enjoy. The smell of redwood forest grew in his nostrils, and the girls' laughter mingled with the Harley-Davidson's powerful rumble. Ahead, the tree-shadowed blacktop opened to the sandy beach where they camped, and he saw brothers waiting near their machines, their smiles wide, fingers raised in greeting peace signs.

He came in fast, listening to the squeals of delight. His right foot came down, and he swung the big motorcycle to a sand-spraying sliding stop.

And . . . Old Dog Carlisle's mind slipped gently into its eternal sleep.

Epilogue

Old Dog's Alaskan letters arrived in Perry County together.

Larry's contained only a hand-drawn map. X marked the spot. Old Dog had delayed sending it until he was sure he could really be there.

Larry tried to imagine his brother lying at peace in the wilderness he so admired. He guessed he could not really share Old Dog's satisfaction. Larry Carlisle's resting place would be with other Carlisle's at home in Perry County, but Old Dog's had been a wild, free roaming spirit that for most had been difficult to understand.

Larry sighed and placed Old Dog's sketch in his lockbox among the living wills and powers of attorney—all of the trappings it took nowadays just to die with a trace of human dignity.

Timmy's Letter was only a note. Except for his signature, Old Dog always printed. The note said:

IT IS WELL WITH ME, TIM. BE GLAD FOR ME.

I LEAVE YOU WITH ONLY TWO OTHER SPECIAL THOUGHTS. NEITHER IS MORE IMPORTANT THAN THE OTHER.

"ENJOY YOUR LIFE, AND DO NOT HARM THE INNOCENT OR THE WORLD DOING SO."

BEYOND THOSE THINGS YOU OWE NOTHING. HELP OTHERS IF YOU WISH, DEDICATE YOUR LIFE TO ANYTHING YOU CHOOSE, BUT ALWAYS OBSERVE THE TWO RULES ABOVE. DO THAT AND YOU WILL NEVER BE SORRY, AND YOUR UNCLE (WATCHING IF THEY ALLOW IT) WILL BE PLEASED FOR YOU.

Old Dog

The End

Made in the USA
Monee, IL
01 September 2021